THE POWER OF
PRESENT

Also by Sirshree

Spiritual Masterpieces - Self Realisation books for serious seekers

Who Am I Now: From mindfulness to no-mind
The Secret of Awakening
100% Karma: Learn the Art of Conscious Karma that Liberates
100% Wisdom: Wisdom that leads you to experience and be established in your true nature
100% Meditation: Dip into the Stillness of Pure Awareness
You are Meditation: Discover Peace and Bliss Within
Essence of Devotion: From Devotee to Divinity
The Unshaken Mind: Discovering the Purpose, Power and Potential of your mind
The Supreme Quest: Your search for the Truth ends there where you are
The Greatest Freedom: Discover the key to an Awakened Living
Secret of The Third Side of The Coin: Unravelling Missing Links in Spirituality
Seek Forgiveness & be Free: Liberation from Karmic Bondage
Passwords to a Happy Life: The Art of Being Happy in all Situations

Self Help Treasures - Self Development books for success seekers

The Source of Health: The Key to Perfect Health Discovery
Inner Ninety Hidden Infinity: How to build your book of values
Inner 90 for Youth: The secret of reaching and staying at the peak of success
The Source for Youth: You have the power to change your life
Inner Magic: The Power of self-talk
Self Encounter: The Complete Path - Self Development to Self Realization
The Five Supreme Secrets of Life: Unveiling the Ways to Attain Wealth, Love and God
You are Not Lazy: A story of shifting from Laziness to Success
Freedom From Fear, Worry, Anger: How to be cool, calm and courageous
The Little Gita of Problem Solving: Gift of 18 Solutions to Any Problem
Freedom From Failure: 7 Spiritual Secrets That Transform Failure Into A Blessing

New Age Nuggets - Practical books on applied spirituality and self help

The Source: Power of Happy Thoughts
Secret of Happiness: Instant Happiness - Here and Now!
Excuse me God...: Fulfilling your wishes through the Power of Prayer and Seed of Faith
Help God to Help You: Whatever you do, do it with a smile
Ultimate Purpose of Success: Achieving Success in all five aspects of life
Celebrating Relationships: Bringing Love, Life, Laughter in Your Relations
Everything is a Game of Beliefs: Understanding is the Whole Thing
Detachment From Attachment: Gift of Freedom From Suffering
Emotional Freedom Through Spiritual Wisdom: How to Take Charge of Your Emotions

Profound Parables - Fiction books containing profound truths

Beyond Life: Conversations on Life After Death
The One Above: What if God was your neighbour?
The Warrior's Mirror: The Path To Peace
Master of Siddhartha: Revealing the Truth of Life and After-life
Put Stress to Rest: Utilizing Stress to Make Progress
The Source @ Work: A Story of Inspiration from Jeeodee

Author of the bestseller *The Source*
SIRSHREE

THE POWER OF
PRESENT

Experience the Joy of the Now

The Power of Present
Experience the Joy of the Now
By Sirshree Tejparkhi

Copyright © Tejgyan Global Foundation
All Rights Reserved 2018

Tejgyan Global Foundation is a charitable organization
with its headquarters in Pune, India.

Published by WOW Publishings Pvt. Ltd., India
First edition published in November 2018

Based on the Hindi book titled 'Vartamaan ka Jaadu'

Copyrights are reserved with Tejgyan Global Foundation and publishing rights are vested exclusively with WOW Publishings Pvt. Ltd. This book is sold subject to the condition that it shall not by way of trade or otherwise, be lent, resold, hired out, or otherwise circulated without the publisher's prior written consent in any form of binding or cover other than that in which it is published and without a similar condition including this condition being imposed on the subsequent purchaser and without limiting the rights under copyright reserved above, no part of this publication may be reproduced, stored in or introduced into a retrieval system, or transmitted, in any form, or by any means, electronic, mechanical, photocopying, recording or otherwise, without the prior written permission of both the copyright owner and the above-mentioned publisher of this book. Any person who does any unauthorized act in relation to this publication may be liable to criminal prosecution and civil claims for damages.

*To the exalted ones
who have transcended the illusion of time
and made the highest use of the eternal present
for the welfare of mankind.*

Contents

Preface   09

PART I - CONTENTMENT IN THE PRESENT

1. The Present is the Key   17
2. The Gift of the Present   24
3. The Art of Being in the Present   31
4. The Window of the Present   42
5. The Feeling of Havingness   47
6. Being Rooted at the Center   51

PART II - FREEDOM FROM PAST AND FUTURE

7. The Secret of the Present   59
8. The Treasure Trove of Happiness   65
9. Relinquishing the Past   70
10. Breaking free from Karmic Bondage   81
11. The Happiness of the Present   86

12. Evaluating Packets 89

13. Dealing with the Past and Future 96

14. Bringing Completeness 101

PART III - HARNESSING THE PRESENT FOR A FULFILLING FUTURE

15. Intuiting the Future 109

16. Receiving Past Parcels Gracefully 115

17. Formula-based Actions 119

18. Starting from the Finishing line 123

Preface

A person, who had reached the end of his life was conversing with God.

> Person: O Lord .. I have many more tasks that are incomplete and wishes that are unfulfilled. I need to prepare a will, take care of my loved ones, witness the birth of my grandchildren.. Please grant me a little more time on earth!
>
> God: My dear child, I am sorry! I cannot grant you that wish. This is the end of your short earthly visit and it is now time for you to continue your onward journey.
>
> Person: *(referring to the suitcase in God's hands)* Why do you carrying this suitcase? What does it contain?
>
> God: This suitcase contains something that belongs to you.
>
> Person: *(happily)* Have you brought me my clothes and my money from earth?
>
> God: The clothes you had in your cupboard and the money you had in the bank, weren't really yours, my child. The clothes that you thought were yours, now belong to those who would wear them. The money that you believed was yours, now belongs to those who would spend it. How then, can you call these things, yours?

Person: Well then, what does this suitcase contain, that belongs to me? Does it contain my relations?

God: The relations you had, were there for you to learn certain lessons. Their sole purpose was to help you discipline yourself, to contemplate and heighten your understanding about life by learning the lessons meant for you. They were there to help you experience the joy of loving and giving. These too, you cannot call yours.

Person: (*bewildered*) If neither the clothes, nor the money, nor the relations are mine, then what does this suitcase contain? Does it contain my skills and abilities?

God: Your skills were meant for and limited to your role on earth. Your abilities were a part of your DNA, which you had inherited from your ancestors. So, these belong to them, not you!

Person: If my skills and abilities do not belong to me either, surely the suitcase contains my memories?

God: The memories are not yours either. They have come to you from past lives.

Person: Neither the memories are mine.. Nor the relations.. Nor the skills... what else remains that could be mine? Does the suitcase contain my body?

God: Your body is made up of the five elements: earth, air, water, fire and space and so it will eventually return to these elements. Your body isn't yours either.

Person: If not my body, does the suitcase contain my soul?

God: Your soul is only a small part of the universal soul, the Divine Being. It does not belong to you either.

Person: Alas! The soul isn't mine either! What else remains that I can call mine?

God: Why don't you open the suitcase and see for yourself?

The person goes on to open the suitcase and is shocked and disappointed to find the suitcase empty.

Person: *(crying bitterly)* It's empty! Does this mean nothing belongs to me? Is there nothing that I can call mine?

God: You're right. Nothing is yours.

Person: O Lord.. there has to be something in the life that I spent on earth, that I can call mine! Please tell me what it is.

The question that the person has asked God is very important and worth contemplating. God replies to him saying:

God: During your life on earth, everything that you accumulated or tried to accumulate was never yours. Life, and everything contained within it, is like a flowing river. You cannot contain it. You cannot accumulate it. But yes, there was something that was yours and that's what is contained in this suitcase. What did belong to you, were the precious moments you lived. All the moments you lived on the earth, were yours.

Understanding this message will help us realize that the present is our true wealth. The present is where the solution exists to every problem, every challenge. This is why it is of vital importance to first learn the art of living in the present.

We have to live every moment to its fullest. We are not to just think about the present moment; we are to live it, imbibe it, be one with it. This skill has to be learnt by every human being. To learn it, we have to learn to return to the present and stay there.

This book is about understanding the importance of being in the present moment and learning how to do it. Being in the present brings a joy that springs from spontaneity and freshness. And the surprising thing is one has to do nothing to experience it. The experience is always already here; we *are* the experience. It's just that it has been shrouded.

This book will go on to show how we are spending too much energy thinking about the past and the future. We just have to stop that and it is all there. One cannot think about being in the present, the way one does about the past and the future. One can just be the present. This being is who you truly are.

These moments that you are present in, just being, are yours. It is these precious moments that make your lifetime worthwhile; and it is these very moments that most people squander away in their preoccupation with the dead past and non-existent future.

This book will serve as a duster, an opener and a periscope. A duster to erase everything that keeps us away from the present. An opener to open our eyes and heart to the present moment that has eluded us so far. And finally, a periscope to help us look at our past and future in the correct, detached and distant way.

While we aim to go beyond the confines of time and realize the essence of our existence, even a small shift in our perception about the present will make this book worthwhile. This small shift will eventually lead to a great spiritual revolution and awakening.

Invest your present in understanding the power of the present, so as to be free from the clutches of the past and create a fulfilling future!

Part I

Contentment in the Present

1

The Present is the Key

Do the following questions ever trouble your mind?

- What direction is my life heading in?
- Why am I not able to control my own actions?
- Why do my thoughts keep running hither and thither?
- Why is my body unhealthy?
- Why does my life feel monotonous and unfulfilled?

If you find yourself plagued by the above questions, it is an indication that you are drifting away from the present. These are symptoms that suggest that you are moving away from the present.

When we drift away from the present, we begin to lead an involuntary and unconscious life. We lose control of our thoughts and actions. This leads to a buildup of negativity in us which affects us on a mental and physical level.

But why do we drift away from the present in the first place?

The answer is quite simple. We drift away from the present because we are afraid of confronting it. We tend to avoid it, and as we keep avoiding it, we get into the habit of living in an unconscious and unaware state. While running away from the present, we never realize when we get addicted to things like alcohol, gambling, excessive eating, shopping, and drugs.

If these vices weren't enough, there are distractions like social media applications - the Whatsapps, Facebooks and Twitters of today. Sure, these platforms can be effectively put to constructive use; but with excessive and indiscriminate indulgence in them, we have allowed our precious moments to be hijacked.

These addictions, in turn, keep pushing us further away from the present. This becomes a vicious cycle that has to be broken. When we learn to do that, we remove all possibilities of letting negativities build up within us. When we are living consciously, when we are in an awakened state, we are in the present.

We humans contain within us both the possibilities: that of rising to divinity and also that of falling to animalistic ways. The path that we choose decides which possibility becomes our reality. Living in an unconscious state takes us away from the present.

When we refuse to stay in the present, we are refusing to be lively; in fact, we are denying life altogether. And when one denies life, one has begun stepping towards death. One may not realize this at the time, but the choice is made and the journey has begun. It is just a matter of time before the inevitable happens.

On the contrary, being in the present opens up the possibilities for attaining divinity. Being aware always keeps our journey going towards spiritual growth, towards eternal life.

But how do we learn to stay in the present? How do we stay in awareness?

There are many ways, but the most simple and straightforward method is that of being a witnesser.

Confronting the present

Whenever you find yourself uncomfortable of confronting the present, assume the role of a witnesser. Witness everything that is happening around you in its entirety. Have the courage to observe exactly what is happening. This gives us the courage to confront the present, and confronting the present will keep us from the entanglements of the past.

Let us say you presently have hundred problems.

You will observe that by making just one or two attempts at being in a self-aware witnessing state during a problem situation, about 20% of the problems begin to move towards solution. Being in the present, elevates our consciousness, which then attracts the best possible solutions to apparently unsolvable problems.

Then you go on to observe that four or five attempts at being in the present will fix another 30% of the problems. Five or six attempts are able to fix nearly 40% more.

These numbers are figurative. They are only meant to illustrate that if we learn to be a witnesser and stay in the present through each and every incident of our life, every problem we have would be fixed. This is how, being a detached witnesser in the present, can be the simplest key to finding the solution for every problem we have.

The fourth eye of faith

The problems we are faced with, strip us of our powers and abilities. Our focus keeps shifting to the problem and we keep obsessing over it. The thoughts of the problem haunt us relentlessly. In such a scenario, we need to open our fourth eye.

But what is the fourth eye?

We know the eyes that we were born with. The third eye, we know, is that of knowledge. What then is the fourth eye?

The fourth eye is the perspective that we achieve by being in the present. It is the eye of the heart. This can also be called the eye of *faith*.

What does this fourth eye enable us to see? It enables us to see something that the two eyes we were born with can't. When we are faced with a problem, the fourth eye helps us see what stands behind the problem. Let us understand this with an example.

Imagine that a fierce enemy of ours comes face to face with us and holds a gun to our head. We are shocked and terrified. This is exactly what happens to us when we come face to face with a problem in life. As soon as our focus shifts to the problem, we are stripped of our energy; we feel weak.

Now, we happen to look past our enemy and what surprise! We see a friend of ours waiting ready, a stick in his hand, ready to strike the enemy! We suddenly feel relaxed and safe. There is nothing to worry anymore. The same enemy who had struck terror in our heart, we greet merrily!

"How are you my dear friend? What brings you here?" we ask.

Now it is the enemy's turn to be shocked! He is astounded by the sudden change in our demeanor. "I am holding a gun and yet this person feels no fear and is talking to me so casually!" The enemy is now afraid of our attitude. This is why it is said that *"When you are unmoved by a situation, the situation moves away."* When your faith remains unshaken, the problem is shaken up. The fourth eye of faith helps us see the friend who is standing behind the problem - ready with a solution.

The fourth eye also helps us understand that *every problem comes bearing gifts.* It is this gift that we need to focus on, not the problem. The true purpose of problems is to bring about growth. Consider them as the precursors to growth and evolution. Problems are not here to trouble us, they are here to help us see something that would otherwise go unnoticed.

We all have within us the ability to harness the power of faith. Problems help us realize that ability. They come with the gift of opportunity. The opportunity for us to develop this ability and make it a habit. When something bad or undesirable is about to happen, our feelings change. We are able to perceive that something has gone wrong on the subtle plane of our feelings.

How does faith function in any situation? Faith tells us exactly how to right the wrong. We have the faculty of intuition too, but intuition only gives us a hint. Faith doesn't just give a hint, it fixes the problem for us, and that too in the best possible way. If we're able to hold on to faith, we realize that whatever happened, wasn't negative. It was a blessing in disguise. This is the power of faith. This is what we have to understand and imbibe by opening the fourth eye. We have to learn to focus on the gift that the problem brings.

By living in the past and leading an unconscious life, we are keeping ourselves in the dark and doused in ignorance. When something hurtful or undesirable happens in the present, we immediately close ourselves down and lose consciousness of the present moment. We are afraid of confronting the present, which takes us away from the state of awareness.

During testing circumstances, the understanding we should have is that if nothing hurtful were to happen to us, we would probably never feel the need to contemplate over the importance of *being* in the present and realize its importance. There would be no growth without hurt and pain. No gain without pain - this is a famous maxim. But the truth is that there is no gain without *understanding* pain. We grow when we gracefully receive and understand what pain has come to teach us.

Consider a movie scene in which the director wants the actor to feel the pain and say certain things, act a certain way and solve a problem in a certain way. When the actor does all these things, the scene is shot the way the director wants and will lead to a complete film as visualized by the director.

Instead, if the actor, afraid of the scene, gets drunk and refuses to work on the scene, how would the scene be shot? It is possible that this very scene was going to bring about a turning point in the film. It is hence essential for the actor (us) to consciously witness the incident that the director (God) wants him to, and confront the present fearlessly and courageously.

With this understanding in focus, let us resolve to always be aware of the present, to just let ourselves be. Let us try and harness as much potential we have of being aware as we can. This very awareness will eventually reveal the biggest secret of the present. The present is the key to all problems, the certain way to be truly happy, successful and content.

2

The Gift of the Present

When we give someone a gift, we insist on them opening the gift in our presence. We want to see them get surprised and happy as they open the gift. We want to see the sparkle in their eyes as they come to know what is packaged inside the gift box.

Quite similarly, we have received a unique gift pack from God that contains 365 smaller gifts. The life that we have been blessed with, gives us 365 gifts every year. God wants us to open every gift with surprise and amazement. He wants us to welcome every moment of the present with open arms and an open mind. Let us make His wish our own and open the gift of the present with the same surprise and excitement that we expect from our friends when we give them gifts.

As we receive the gift of the Present, He observes that our focus, instead of being on opening the gift, is drifting elsewhere. Instead of seeing amazement for the present moment in our eyes, He sees tears of sorrow for the past or apprehension about the future. This is why it becomes necessary to train ourselves to greet the present with wonder and amazement. Life is amazing. It is magical. Every moment of life is packed with fascination and wonderment. Let us learn to look at life with this perspective.

The eye of wonder

A twenty year old boy was travelling with his father in a train. The boy was sitting by the window and his father sitting next to him. The train left the station and was soon passing through the beautiful countryside.

As the train chugged along, the boy was enjoying the beautiful sceneries outside the window. He would excitedly describe whatever he was seeing to his father. The lush green trees, the straw huts, the gushing rivers, bridges and valleys - nothing missed his eye! He described with wonder how the trees and the mountains were moving along with the train. The father was enjoying his son's descriptions too, peeping outside the window every now and then, looking at whatever his son pointed at.

An elderly person sitting next to the father was feeling weird about this behavior of a twenty year old boy. He felt the excitement to be quite unnatural for a boy that old. After suppressing his curiosity for a long time, the elderly person finally asked the father about his son's behavior.

The father smiled and said, "I can understand why you think his excitement is unnatural, but I also know that it isn't wrong. My son has been blind since his birth and only now, after twenty years of darkness, has he got his eyesight. For that reason, everything that looks commonplace to you, is a fresh experience for him. He is seeing all these beautiful things for the first time in his life and hence his excitement!"

Now, not only the elderly gentleman who had asked the question, but everyone else in that train compartment who had heard the answer, looked at the boy and at the scenes outside the window with a new perspective.

When we experience something beautiful for the first time, we are able to savor it thoroughly. However, having experienced it once, the subsequent encounters feel dull and boring.

Have you observed children? How are they able to be so happy and uninhibited all the time? Because they live every moment in wonder and amazement. If you give a child a mobile phone, he is amazed at how he is able hear someone without seeing them! He is amazed that the little device in his hands is able to play songs and even show pictures! But if someone were to ask us, "Do you feel amazed about the mobile phone?", we'll probably say, "Not really! What's the big deal?!". And yet, we as children have also wondered at things.

This quality of looking at things with amazement that we had in our own childhood, has waned with time. Through this book, we are going back into the world of amazement, where we marvel at even the simplest thing like a radio. It is ironic that in this age of technological advancement, when we are surrounded by incredible devices and concepts, while we have so much around us to marvel at, we've lost the ability to wonder. The ability to wonder at every little thing, having the eye that looks for amazement in everything, can give us boundless happiness.

Being in the present and living every moment with wonderment not only saves us a lot of energy, but also gives us more of it. It adds to our happiness. In the absence of the understanding of how happiness is multiplied we would think, "If I am to give away all the happiness I have now, how will I find happiness for myself in the times to come?".

These are the thoughts coming from the limited intelligence of the brain. This makes us a miser at spreading love and happiness. On the contrary, if we have abundance of happiness ourselves and we know the secret to finding more, we would generously give out happiness to everyone, thus also elevating their energy levels.

For example, when we're listening to someone talk with all our attention, the other person's energy level grows. Energy is getting transferred from us to the person who is talking to us, and it doesn't cause us much discomfort either, because by learning to live in the present, we have tapped into the source of infinite energy. Thus, we can generously give out energy.

Conversely, when we're not able to live in the present, we feel drained of energy and are consequently not able to give out any. In other words, when we are not living in the present, we're not enabling others either. Let us try and understand this further with a story which, although imaginary, points to a very important fact:

> Once upon a time, there lived a boy named Alex. Alex was always unhappy and complaintive about his present situation.
>
> One fine day, he decided to voice his dissatisfaction to God.

"When will this change?" he said to God. "When will I grow up and get to live on my own terms?"

God heard his plea and granted him a boon. "I have heard your woes, my child, and I have decided to bestow upon you, a boon. Whenever you are faced with a situation you dislike, you can snap your fingers and jump to the next scene."

Alex was very happy with this boon and got back to living his life.

A few days later, his exams were about to begin and it was high time for Alex to start preparing for it. He was extremely bored of studying and was thinking of ways to escape it. Just then, he remembered the boon. Happy to have finally found the escape, he snapped his fingers and jumped to the vacation that followed the exams!

Alex was now happily enjoying his vacation, just when a new curiosity gripped him: "Which place would we visit on the annual trip this year?" Curiosity got the better of him and he snapped his fingers again to jump to the trip!

Alex was barely able to enjoy living in the present. Thanks to the boon, he just kept snapping away to the next scene, avoiding everything he disliked or found boring. Even during vacations, he kept jumping to the next scene, getting bored all the time. With this tendency of escaping the present, he had made the boon into a curse.

A time came when Alex started finding every situation boring, always finding himself saying "What next?" and snapping his fingers and jumping ahead. Even a little discomfort, and snap!

Subsequently, Alex kept snapping ahead and jumped to the time when he got married and had kids. Whenever he came across a situation where his wife would berate him, he would snap and jump ahead. Soon, he had jumped right across his life and reached the end!

"Alas," he realized, "I did not get to live my life at all! I kept jumping to the next scene, never really living the moment I had in front of me, and here I am, at death's door, never having truly lived at all!"

Do you feel sorry for poor Alex and for what happened to him? You'll be surprised to know that Alex's story is in fact, our story!

Alex represents our mind, which is used to running away from the present situation to avoid any confrontation and discomfort. The mind wants to live either in the past or in the future - whether that leads to happiness or sorrow, comfort or fear, is immaterial for the mind. It will feel remorseful about the past. It will wish that things hadn't happened the way they did. It will want to entertain itself with past memories and want to relive them. It fears for the future. It fantasizes about it.

The mind just wants to find the quickest way to escape the present and get as far away from it as possible. This tendency of the mind steals the joy of simply living each moment and enjoying every experience in its raw form. While something wonderful could be happening in the present, the mind is worried about what would come next. This is how the present keeps slipping away from us.

Let us contemplate on what we have learnt in this chapter and apply it to our lives. Let us train ourselves to focus on the present moment, to experience the fresh present, because the secret is that it is only in the present that we can find the key to true happiness.

3

The Art of Being in the Present

Once upon a time, in some kingdom, a king organized a competition which was won by a village chieftain. In addition to receiving a lot of gifts from the king, he also received a gleaming trophy. A year later, the chieftain decided to organize the same competition in his village.

To prepare for the competition, he had to buy some things from the market, for which he set out with his son.

His son was suffering from poor eyesight and had to keep washing his eyes with water very often, and even then he was barely able to see enough.

While they were on their way to the market, the chief met an acquaintance whom he explained the reason for his visit to the market.

"I am organizing the same competition that I had won the trophy for last year", he said.

"When did you win the trophy?" his friend asked, surprised. "As far as I remember, no one won the trophy last year!"

The proud village chieftain was shocked at his words. "I will ask for the trophy to be brought here to show you, if you don't believe me!".

Saying this, the chief asked his son to go home and fetch the trophy from the showcase in the drawing room. Meanwhile, at the chief's home, the servant had taken the trophy from the showcase, cleaned it and kept it on a table.

The son reached home and searched for the trophy all over the place, but being poor sighted, he wasn't able to find it. He saw the trophy on the table, but wan't able to recognize it as the very trophy he'd been looking for. Instead, he mistook the trophy to be an eye-cup. He poured water into it and rinsed his eyes. The son then returned to his father, carrying the trophy with him, still considering it as an eye-cup.

"Father, I looked for the trophy everywhere, but I couldn't find it", he informed his father unhappily.

While the son was upset about not having found the trophy, his father was surprised about him being upset, because he could clearly see him holding the very trophy that he was sent to fetch!

Let us try and understand the underlying message that this little story conveys. The trophy represents the joy of being in the present. But like the son, we too are not able to see the trophy that is with us all the time. We keep thinking, "Why is my life devoid of happiness? Why isn't my mind at peace?"

While we all have the source of abundant happiness, right here within us, we are looking for it elsewhere, complaining all the time about how we are always deprived of happiness and peace. Isn't it ironic that just like the son in the story, we too are looking everywhere for something that is always in our own hands! It is like a fish swimming around searching for water. If the source of happiness is within us, it makes common sense in looking within, not without!

Our mind has trained itself to look at every incident and person in a set way. It has a very limited perspective about things and sticks to that perspective in judging everything it sees. This very habit of the mind becomes a trap for itself. Like a spider that cannot help building a web around itself and finally getting stuck in the middle of it, the mind cannot help creating this web that it gets trapped in, taking a lifetime to get out of it, seldom finding the way out.

As humans, being happy and peaceful is our basic nature. Happiness is the core of our being, and yet we are driven away from this state which is necessarily our most intrinsic attribute. Isn't it surprising how something so plain and obvious as the sky in broad daylight, gets shrouded by the clouds of ignorance?

The sky of the present is constantly lit up by the sun of happiness and contentment. Just the way during the day, the presence of sunlight is a given, likewise, while we're being in the present, the presence of happiness and contentment are a given! But we're lost to the clear skies of the present, because we are too accustomed to looking at everything the way our mind tells us to, without questioning its ways.

The labels of the mind

Our mind has a tendency of labelling everything – people, situations and incidents. With time and conditioning, it has grown incapable of looking at things the way they actually are, *without labelling them.*

Let us once again turn to observing little children and learn from their behavior. How do one or two year old children look at things? They look at everything with a fresh perspective, as if they have come across it for the first time. Notice how kids receive us every day. They receive us as if they are seeing us for the first time, and they do it with the same enthusiasm every day! How?

Because they are free of labels. Their mind hasn't developed the habit of labelling things. If we scold them, they do not label us as "atrocious" and look at us with hate every time they see us. They do not form opinions about things and they do not categorize experiences as good or bad, less or more. Everything that comes their way is seen (received) with a fresh and unstamped perspective.

Observe kindergarten kids. Do they seem to be happier on Fridays because they're on the brink of the weekend or sad on a Sunday evening because the weekend is over? Have they labelled the weekend as *good* and weekdays as *bad*? No. Let us contemplate on our own feelings on Friday and Sunday evenings. How do we look at the same things that kids do? What stops us from viewing something that is new or unfamiliar, just the way it truly is? How is our perspective different from theirs?

Even a little puppy on the road gets a kid excited. We on the other hand, see nothing novel about it. We tend to slap a label on everything. We feel the compulsive need to classify and categorize. We put people and incidents into neat little boxes with labels on them. The box restricts our perspective for them.

Whatever they are in reality, for us they mean only what the label reads.

Just the way we have a box and a *label* for everything around us, we have one for ourselves too. We think of ourselves as the label and eventually feel pigeonholed into that idea. We proceed down that path without ever challenging the notion.

We need to change this. When we decide to describe ourselves or anything else, let's get beyond labels. We have to learn to see things *as-they-are*. We have to view ourselves, our surroundings, situations, events and people with a fresh perspective, discarding all recordings of the past.

It is only by viewing them from a fresh perspective that we will be able to spread love to everyone, and a fresh perspective can be gained only by discarding all labels. Old perceptions will carry old impressions drawn from the experiences of the past. We have to search within for the existence of any such impressions and let go of them.

The same applies to relationships too. Consider the relationship between any two people; friends, spouses, colleagues etc. During the initial days of the relationship, their minds are free of presumptions and biases. Due to the absence of preconceived ideas, there is love and understanding. However, as days pass by, as they get to know each other's habits and behaviors, they unknowingly start forming impressions about each other. They begin to assume the words and reactions of the other person and the love and understanding soon begins to fades away.

If we interact with people by holding the same old perspective we have of them, we will only reap what we always have from the relationship. For something new to happen, we have to change the perspective, get rid of past impressions and receive them newly, as if we are meeting them for the very first time. The best way to have great relationships in life is to remove the past from all the relationships, enabling us to welcome everyone with a fresh outlook.

Seeing the unseen

There are many things around us that are truly marvelous, yet, just because they have become a part of our mundane existence, we take them for granted and fail to appreciate their true glory. For example, the beauty of a cloudy sky on a rainy day, the beautiful colors that fill up the sky on a sunny evening. How many times have we stepped out in the open, looked up at the sky and marveled at the beauty that meets the eye? It is unfortunate that we choose to see all these things on a television instead of stepping out and experiencing it firsthand!

Imagine a painter painting a scene, in which he has painted grass in a beautiful shade of green. He then uses black to give the grass blades an outline, which gives it a 3D effect. When we look at the finished painting, we are not directly looking at the black color, but we love the 3D effect that the grass has. That effect is owing to the black color. The color is doing its job! It is only when we look at the painting with the eyes of a painter that we can see the existence of the black color. In the absence of that vision, we will only take the existence of the back color for granted.

Likewise, everything that nature has shaped around us, whether it is people, situations or incidents, are all beautiful and marvelous, just the way they are. The key to being infinitely happy is to learn to look at them afresh while staying in the present, without labelling them.

Refreshing our perception

Looking at things afresh means renewing our experience of them. Refreshing the perspective we have of them. To witness something by experiencing it. The joy in experiencing something as-it-is from a renewed perspective is like the brilliance of sunlight in comparison to the dull candlelight of the old lens of beliefs and packets that we are used to seeing through.

Imagine we're out on a picnic to a beautiful place, full of natural beauty. We're surrounded by trees, flowers, little streams, foggy mountains and deep valleys. When we are amongst them, we actually look at them, feel them and *experience* their beauty; we don't just *think* about them.

But are these things new to us? Have we never seen trees and rivers and mountains before? We have! And yet we experience them with renewed interest; with a fresh perspective. The goal is to adopt the same attitude for everything else in life: people, events and incidents. We have to learn to experience them afresh; even those we have already experienced before without labelling them. Dropping the habit of sticking labels on our experiences is the key here.

Let us reminisce the times when we used to enjoy the rains as kids. We would spend hours looking out of the window, watching the trees, the street, the house roof getting wet. The earthy scent that would invade the air. How the raindrops would fall drop by drop, forming puddles. How we loved getting drenched in the rain, feeling the cold rain water on our skin. Now, let us come back to the present. Are we able to enjoy the monsoons the same way? The words "Oh, its raining!", that were once uttered with joy, are now uttered with disgust. As adults we've slapped a label on everything.

Something that used to be a beautiful experience is now a hindrance, a nuisance. Instead of enjoying this beautiful natural phenomenon, we grumble about too much or too little rain, we worry about how the roads will be filled with traffic and how we will catch a cold if we get drenched.

It is only when we learn to absorb these experiences while being in the present moment, that we will grasp the key to being truly happy. This is the power of the present - it holds the key to happiness. Neither the elapsed nor the eventual can give you permanent and unbroken bliss. It is only being in the present moment and the ability to take everything *as it is* - without labelling - that can give us the truly lasting happiness that we all crave for.

Open the window to the present and live it every moment. Let life unfold in the present. Do not let the present slip away, allowing time to rush past unobserved and unseized, and squandering the precious moments of our lives worrying about the future and ruminating about the past.

Breathing meditation

We have been breathing ever since we were born and shall continue till the last day of our earthly existence. Our body knows how to breathe without needing any conscious control on our part. It is an involuntary, automatic task that it performs day in and day out.

However, how many times have we paid attention to something so vital going on in our body? We tend to ignore this vital life-giving aspect, until we are met with a dearth of it. Ask someone who is struggling for breath, and he would give away anything he has, just for getting back his breath!

Isn't it amazing that the very thing that keeps us alive, is the most neglected thing ever?! We are detached from our breath. We have no label for it. We do not think of our breathing as either good or bad, relaxing or taxing, deep or shallow.

If one were to have the same detachment from thoughts as one has from breathing, it would be immensely easier to master the mind. Because of this direct link between our breathing and our mental state, the former has an important place in mind-control. Breathing can become the key to bring us into the present; it helps us empty ourselves; create a vacuum within.

Empty ourselves of what? Of thoughts. The traffic of thoughts, is an obstruction to being in the present. We are so full of thoughts, that we leave no room for anything new or different to enter our lives. We are aware of the natural law that wherever there is vacuum, air rushes in to fill up that space. When we empty ourselves of our thoughts, we create a vacuum within and everything that we need and wish for, begins to flow in, automatically with effortless ease. It only remains for us to learn how to empty ourselves.

Breathing meditation is an effective method to slowly power down the mind and enter a thoughtless space. To do that, bring your awareness to your breathing. Wherever you are, standing or sitting, in a car, at home or at work, consciously bring your focus to the cycle of inhalation and exhalation.

Because you breathe automatically, you don't normally pay attention to breathing. This is an opportunity to become more aware of the nature of your breath. As you become aware of your breathing, don't try to consciously change it. Having an awareness of your breath and an acceptance of how it is without trying to change it is a perfect example of mindfulness.

Just follow your breath without trying to regulate or change it. When your lungs want to breathe in, allow it. When your lungs want to breathe out, allow it. If there is a pause between your exhalation and inhalation, that's okay too. Rest in the stillness of that pause. Just witness whatever happens, as it happens.

Analyze your breath.

Observe whether your breath is deep or shallow.

Is it quiet or loud?

Is it short or long?

Is it tight or relaxed?

Do you feel the act of breathing mostly in your belly, chest, nose, or somewhere else?

Do your in-breath and out-breath take the same time?

Become curious!

With this exercise, you will notice that the turbulent waters of the mind become still. Every time you feel overwhelmed by thoughts, take a moment and do the breathing meditation to restore calmness and return to the present. We have to learn to observe thoughts the way we observe our breathing; without labels and with detachment.

The traditional practice of fasting

Hunger is another feeling that can help us stay in the present. Hunger is felt by our body in the present moment. It is a physical phenomenon felt on the physical plane. It acts as an anchor to keep us tethered to the present. When our body isn't spending energy digesting food, our internal organs can adapt and start producing the essential nutrients we previously were getting from our food. Over time, we begin tapping into how the physical body feels and learn to read it on a deeply connected level.

It allows us to distinguish where certain desires come from, whether they are a product of our ego or a calling from the true self. We become aware of our attachments to food either as a distraction or a mechanism to feel better. This allows us to take control of our spiritual will and to not be subject to the desires of the physical realm.

4

The Window of the Present

Who doesn't like open windows?! Whether it is a window of opportunity or whether it is just a window in the wall, we like it to be open. We like it to be a source of fresh air and beautiful landscapes. The present can be looked upon as a window. Moreover, it the *only* window that is open at any given moment! This window gives you access to the experience of the ultimate truth and is a source of fresh breeze that comes from looking at everything with a renewed perspective. Like the fresh breeze, the window of the present is alive and conscious.

The past on the other hand is only an illusion of a window. Imagine a picture hung up on the wall. It is a picture of an open window overlooking a beautiful scenery. Howsoever beautiful the scenery and howsoever wide open the window may be, it is still just a picture, an illusion. The past is like this picture. It is only an illusion of an open window and a beautiful scene. It might make you happy, but the happiness would be shortlived and shallow. It is dead and gone and exists only as pictures in our memory. Upon the disruption of this illusion, we realize the fact that the present is the only open window, giving you fresh air and oxygen, necessary for your survival.

This same window of the present also holds the key to the window of the future. Hence, by shifting your focus to the window of the present, you not only grasp the essence of eternal happiness but also unlock the prospects of the future.

A single open window that has the potential to deliver so much, is surely important and worth all your attention! Only by living in the present, by taking every moment as an incredible wonder, will we be able to unlock the future with the key of *'wait, watch and wonder'*. Staying in the past, focusing your attention on the illusory window of the bygone will only take you farther from this understanding.

Why do people feel powerless and listless? Why do they feel drained out even without doing much physical work?

The resentments about the past and the anxiety about the future suck the energy of the present moment. This is the reason most people feel devoid of energy most of the time. People who practice being in the present are able to harness this energy and channelize it in the right direction. So much that even at the end of a hectic day they feel energetic and enthusiastic.

The vacillating mind keeps our focus engaged on either the past or the future - in short everywhere else except where it should be! It always tends to focus on negatives that form an illusory world around us, and as per the law, whatever we focus on, is attracted into our life.

Consequently, it is our vacillating and judging mind that is the real reason behind us attracting negativity into our lives time and again. Understanding this through the experiences of our own lives causes the vacillating, judging and discriminating tendencies of the mind to vanish and we begin to see wonders around us - wonders that have always been there, but which were lost to us, due to our preoccupation with our own judgments and preconceived notions .

Being mindful (by having a curious, non-expecting, intentional attention on the present) annihilates the vacillating tendency of the mind. We live in peaceful acceptance of the natural way that life unfolds in the present.

As we begin the practice of staying in the present, it might feel difficult to find amazement in every moment. However, with persistence, we can get trained to find wonderment everywhere. Musical notes make no sense unless we train ourselves to read them. Likewise we have to train ourselves to marvel at every moment. Life then becomes an endless series of wonders.

With time and persistence, this practice seeps down to all our senses and we tap into the eternal source of love, happiness and peace. Living in the present, our effort springs from a state of peace without judgment; such effort takes the nature of effortless effort, devoid of struggle and conflict.

Wherever we may be - at work, at home or travelling to some place - we can live in wonder. We get rid of the tendency of labelling everything as good or bad, gain or loss, attractive or ugly. With the loss of this tendency, there remains nothing for the vacillating and judging mind to do, and it steps down.

Whatever we choose to focus on, shapes our future. If we focus on problems, we will find them in the future. If we choose peace, that's what our future will hold. Our beliefs become our prayers and the prayers of today become manifestations of tomorrow. Hence, by learning to focus on the present moment, not only are we deriving true happiness but also unlocking a future full of prospects.

Grief is only one of the many alternatives

Certain examinations have multiple choice type questions and students have to choose the correct alternative to score marks. Likewise, when we encounter incidents in life, or when we interact with people, we are given multiple choices. Grief is only one of them. Unfortunately, due to the preconceived formulae of the past, sorrow is perceived as inevitable, rather than as an alternative.

Feeling sorrow after an unpleasant incident is only one of the choices we can make. We can either choose sorrow, or we can choose to immediately shift focus to our breathing and find tranquility in the space of the present.

Okay, but tomorrow!

We have seen how staying in the present, helps us channelize our energy in the right direction and also leads us to saving a lot of it, making us feel energetic all the time. When we tell ourselves, "Let me look at the present moment. Let me see what exactly is happening right now.", we are automatically brought to the present, making us receptive to everything that is happening around us.

At such a time, while being in the moment, we might find that our mind is complaining about the present situation like the traffic, the rain; anything undesirable: "There is so much traffic on the road, I wish the roads were less jammed!", "Why did my project get rejected?! I wish it were approved."

When we find ourselves in such situations, our mind will tend to obsess over the situation, overthinking about it, spending a lot of energy. During such times, to quell the mind's jabbering and save energy, one should tell oneself, "Okay, but tomorrow!".

"I wish the roads were less jammed... Okay, but tomorrow!"

"I wish my project was selected... Okay, but tomorrow!"

As soon as we say these words, we will notice that the vacillating mind quiets down; making way for things to take a natural course, and unfold what is best for us. The energy we save as a result of this, also gets channelized in the right way; it becomes an investment for the future. As we practice this, we will begin to realize that the things we wished would happen, actually do happen in the future.

When we tell the mind, "Okay, but tomorrow!" we are accepting the present situation as it is, and laying the foundation of a future where our wishes get manifested.

5

The Feeling of Havingness

The present moment is a gift and just like any other gift we receive, all it takes is for us to open and enjoy it. Unfortunately instead of opening the gift of the present, we indulge in the memories of the past.

Whatever happens in the present will soon transform into memories of the past, and owing to the tendency of never being in the present, that is what we end up doing in the future too. We are stuck in a vicious cycle.

For example, an associate who is going to be a manager in his future, thinks, "I will never be as controlling and dictatorial as my manager!" and the manager who was once an associate thinks, "I was never as inefficient and incompetent as my associate!". The manager was once an associate and the associate will someday be a manager. So instead of finding faults with each other, they should dedicate their energy and attention to their present state of being and find happiness therein. By giving all their focus and attention to the present, they would be laying the foundation of a wonderful future.

By clinging onto the past, we end up re-creating it in our future. Our present, past and the future all look alike. We make the same mistakes and attract the same kinds of people and situations - all simply because our focus is in the wrong place.

A person who tends to stay obsessed with either the past or the future, ends up feeling drained of energy and depressed all the time. This depression soon gives way to frustration and thereby to suppressed anger and resentment. The person develops an irritable behavior and has frequent outbursts of anger. The outburst however, doesn't resolve the anger in the person, and it starts building up again the very next moment until it erupts again. This cycle of depression, frustration, resentment and anger drives the person further away from the present.

To save ourselves from this cycle, we have to learn to always adopt the perspective of abundance, to be a "have" as against being a "have-not". For this, we have to first learn to make the most of the present. This present moment is complete in itself. The happiness that it can deliver has no dependencies or prerequisites. We can choose to be happy right here, right now.

Realizing the importance of what we have today

If someone were to ask us, "What would you give to resurrect your beloved ones?", our answer almost certainly would be "Whatever it takes!". If we are ready to do whatever it takes for people who have passed away, what would be the quantum of things we should be prepared to do for the ones who are with us in the present?

We dearly miss the people and the belongings we have lost, but how much do we value the ones we have today? How much do we value our health in the present? Looking at these possessions from the perspective of the present moment will help us realize their importance.

If something has to be done for them, it has to be in the present. Tomorrow after we have lost them, we shall be prepared to do whatever it takes; pay whatever price; to get them back. Of the many benefits of being in the present and focusing on the now, one is the realization of the importance of all that we have today.

Whatever we do – read, work, drive, cook, clean – let us savor the act and feel the joy it produces. Close your eyes for a moment and ask yourself, "Is this moment full of joy and wonder?" Feel the moment before you answer that and you will find that the answer shifts you to the perspective of abundance, of havingness.

Most of us tend to adopt the very opposite of this perspective – that of scarcity. Most people squander away their lifetime by being a have-not. When this feeling of scarcity is at the root of our actions, the outcome will obviously be negative, and the negative outcomes further reinforces the feeling of being a have-not.

With the perspective of abundance, however, you will notice that positive things manifest effortlessly and in a natural free flow. Let us understand this further from the following example:

> *Jim had been desperately looking for a job for a long time and had applied in many places for one. The primary thought in his mind though was that "I do not have a job! I am not receiving positive responses from anywhere!" Then one day,*

he received a call from one of the places that he had applied at, telling him that he had been selected for the job! He was overjoyed. He finally had a job!

As it happened, in the days that followed, he received responses from other places that he had applied at, telling him that he had cleared the interviews there as well!

How did this happen? What brought about these manifestations?

When Jim received the first positive reply, he was shifted from a perspective of scarcity to that of abundance, from a have-not to a have. This shift in perspective was what brought about the magic.

Consider the example of a woman who is not able to conceive. The predominant thought in her mind is "I am not able to conceive. I do not have a child." Then someone suggests her to adopt a child. She does that and the thought changes to "I have a child!" and shortly thereafter, she conceives.

Such is the wonderful magic of the feeling of havingness. When we establish ourselves in this feeling, nature helps dissolve all our problems. All challenges seem to automatically find miraculous solutions.

Staying in the present moment and perceiving every person and incident with the feeling of abundance and havingness is an art that is worth the effort to inculcate. Let neither the past nor the future overshadow the present moment. Stay in the moment and discover the boundless ocean of joy that it is.

6

Being Rooted at the Center

There is a natural and ever-present state of peace and happiness within us. When we are in that state, nothing can shake us. Some people refer to this as 'being in the zone'. Others call this 'inner serenity', which is beyond the highs and lows of pleasure and pain. This natural state is the experience of consciousness. It is the experience of Being.

When this experience is accessed, there is a flow of abundance and serenity in life. If we are unable to experience this natural state of being in our everyday humdrum, it is because the experience has been obscured by the curtains of ignorance.

Let us first dispel this ignorance by briefly delving into what this experience is like.

When our 'Being' is experienced, the oneness behind everything becomes evident. This experience is beyond concepts; it exists beyond thoughts. Hence, *thinking* about the experience of 'Being' has nothing to do with actually experiencing it. Thoughts have nothing to do with 'Being'; they are in fact a hindrance to it.

We hear people say, "This is from my heart", "I wrote from my heart", "All my compositions simply flow from my heart", "I am going with the flow", and so on. What are they referring to? They are referring to an inner experience which comes from the seat of 'Being', which is beyond the knowledge of the mind.

This experience is beyond the language of the mind. When this is experienced, the miracles that emerge will make you wonder. "How did such a composition take shape? Such compositions never emerged before!" When a poet composes an exquisite piece of poetry, he himself is amazed. He wonders, 'How did such poetry emerge from within me!' The poet knows the words, but not how to combine and compose them.

This creativity comes from Being - the source of everything. As soon as he moves away from the clamor of thoughts, as soon as he transcends his mind and reaches the heart, such compositions begin to emerge.

This experience of Being is the very essence of our existence and knowingness. But where is it connected to the human body? It is roughly in the area of the heart. However, this is not the physical heart. It is the subtle place where the formless reality unites with the physical form. It is called the subtle place, because it is not actually a location that can be physically pointed out. This is the seat of inner experience.

When we reach the seat of our 'Being', we access our original state. This state is like a gateway into the present, which brings liberation from past impressions and the anxieties or imaginations of the future. It brings liberation from misery. It is just in the present - not in the head, but in the heart.

By being present in the natural experience of 'Being' and operating from there, you are helping your heart to take over your life. Whenever you have to make a decision, dive within and consult your heart. You shall receive guidance from within; directly from the source, from consciousness – the all-knowing principle that permeates the universe.

We need to learn the art of connecting to our center. Whenever we are faced with any problem or want to decide something, we should close our eyes and shift to the heart. The message you are sending to the universe is that you are ready and willing to receive guidance. Guidance will then automatically flow from the heart.

In order to remain rooted at the center, we need to constantly keep a check on any drift towards the content of thoughts. One who is always alert alone can remain at the center; the one who is not aware, tends to gravitate towards the world of myriad thoughts and remain stuck there.

The drift away from the heart towards the realm of thoughts makes us lose our awareness. As a result, even the simplest tasks appear difficult. We hold onto thoughts and get lost in the train of thoughts that follow. But no sooner do we let go of our thoughts, than we find ourselves at our center; at the root of our 'being'.

Holding onto anything is 'doing' and letting go of everything is 'being'. Here, nothing needs to be 'done' to let go. Nothing could be easier than accessing the heart. Even breathing and blinking one's eyes is 'doing' which is more engaging than effortless 'being'.

Let us understand this with an example. Suppose that a man is standing in front of you, thinking about something. He is lost in the drift of his own thoughts. Even if he is looking at you, you know that he is immersed in his own thoughts and will only snap out of his reverie if you do something to distract him.

Similarly, suppose you are standing in front of the mirror, lost in your own drift of thoughts. It is easy to come out of it if someone just waves a hand in front of you. In the same way, man gets lost in his imagination and does not return to reality.

Even though coming back to reality or awareness is the easiest thing of all, it becomes difficult. The utter simplicity of just 'being' is difficult for the mind as anything the mind can conceive or imagine is far more complex and farfetched.

Great achievements are possible when we connect with the heart instead of focusing on thoughts. This is because consciousness always expresses its creative potential through bodies that are receptive. New ideas can be launched and innovations can be manifested.

Many marvelous creations are waiting to manifest on Earth, but people are not yet ready for them. When people learn to access the heart, only then will those things be able to manifest on Earth.

Self-enquiry in the present

To develop the ability to be rooted in the present, one should persistently engage in self-enquiry. However dense the clouds of illusion that surround one may be, self-enquiry is the way to shatter them and reach the pristine light of our pure consciousness.

When an incident evokes negative feelings, many of us try to immediately escape the incident and brood. It is important to identify such moments as they are the perfect times to ask yourself who you really are and who is the one feeling grief about the situation.

Everything in this world has a role to play; even the negatives. Everything negative is meant to remind us of the positive. The presence of valleys uplifts the presence of hills. The presence of black uplifts the value of white. Every negative incident comes as opportunity to realize our true self; our true potential.

Sorrow, grief, disappointment, anger are all emotions and we need to understand who is the one experiencing these. They are colors that are being used to paint a picture, but who is the painter? When we use grief to know more about ourselves, we turn grief into a ladder to rise to a higher state of being.

When you ask yourself, "Exactly what is happening and with whom?" in any situation, the mind will first throw up readymade obvious answers: "I am upset; it's me." But then we can probe the validity of these obvious thoughts: "What exactly is it like to be 'upset'? What's the sensation? Where is it being felt on the body? How intense is it? And if it's happening with 'me', where is this 'me'? Is it in the head, or elsewhere?"

The moment you investigate the validity of what is being felt and the truth about who exactly is feeling it, it begins to lose its grip on you. With this, it becomes easier to gain stability and abide in the present.

Peace and happiness is our true nature. We do not have *to do anything* to be happy; on the contrary being anything else other than our true self needs energy. We feel tired and depleted because we squander an alarming amount of energy *not being ourselves!* However, as soon as we remind ourselves, we can return to our true nature. We not only save a lot of energy, but by attaining a higher state of being, we can also radiate the energy to those around us.

Part II

Freedom from Past and Future

7

The Secret of the Present

Time is a linear concept. In the context of time, events occur in a chronological order; one after the other. The words 'before' and 'after' are the linear facets of time. We perceive the manifest world and everything therein, on the basis of time. For us, everything is either a part of the past, the present, or the future.

However, the concept of time cannot explain what exists beyond time. We need to go beyond time, to understand what lies therein.

Consider a timeline drawn on a paper; a line with an arrow to its right as shown below:

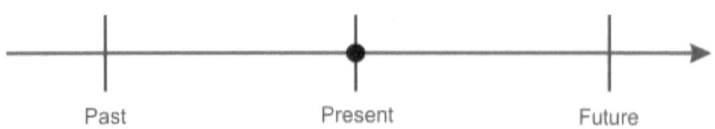

On this timeline, we believe that the past is followed by the present and the present is followed by the future. These three tenses of time appear to be in this chronological order. This itself a great illusion and therein lies the secret of present.

The present is *not* a point in time as is apparent from the above figure. The present is *space*.

The present moment is just a window into the eternal and spacious present. The present transcends the concept of time; it is omnipresent and it is the one that contains everything. Let us try to understand this with the help of the following analogy:

On the paper on which we have drawn the timeline, let us make a little hole at the point where it says "Present". This hole goes through the paper and one is able to see through the paper into what is beyond. The hole represents the *present moment* that is the window to enter the space that lies beyond the hole; beyond the paper. This space is what the present really is. It contains the past and the future. It contains the very paper on which we have drawn the timeline. It transcends time and every phenomenon that depends on it. It is the eternal present which contains the past, the future, and also this present moment.

If you were to stack the film of a bunch of pictures together, you wouldn't be able to make sense when the whole stack is viewed as once. Hence, you introduce a gap in viewing each individual film, before moving onto the next one in sequence. This helps in making sense out of what is being seen. This gap is called 'time'.

Linear time - however wonderful an invention it maybe - is just a mechanism that helps us put things in an order, a sequence to understand them better. It is necessary for the logical progress of the material world.

However, time is a projection on the eternal unbounded canvas of the present. It exists because of and within the present. The past - a memory - and the future - an imagination - are facets of this projection; and both exist merely as thoughts.

However, can one find the past anywhere? Can one clutch the future, however hard one tries? No! Neither the past nor the future have an independent and tangible existence. They are merely thoughts. If today is Wednesday, Tuesday is the past and Thursday is the future. And yet, these are just thoughts. They are inventions of time, meant for our convenience. Without a Wednesday, neither a Tuesday nor a Wednesday would exist.

The present, however, exists beyond the realm of thoughts. Hence, when we try to capture the present in our thoughts, it eludes us. One can think about the present, but it is not the same as experiencing the present. One can either think about it, or actually "be" there. The mind says, "Let me capture the present. Let me see what it feels like", and this *thought* itself becomes an obstacle to being in the present! The thought is not the experience; rather, the thought is "about" the experience.

The present is not a point between the past and the future. It is the space of awareness that contains thoughts of the past and the future. This divine space is where God, the True Self, pure consciousness lives.

Consciousness chooses to invest its attention in thoughts of the past or the future - that is to say, evoke the respective thought. These thoughts arise in our awareness - this very awareness is the present. In other words, thoughts of the past and the future appear in our conscious awareness, which is the timeless present.

When a flare is shot up in the sky, it glows for a while and then dissolves in the sky. The past, the future, memories, imaginations, are all like flares that are projected in the sky of awareness. This space *contains* the flares. We experience the timeless present when we look at thoughts for what they truly are, without focusing on the content of the thoughts.

Once we have understood that the past, the future and the concept of time that encompasses them are all thoughts that have appeared in awareness, the next step is to go beyond and understand where these thoughts come from.

Consciousness is the source of thoughts. It is the wellspring from which the stream of thoughts originates. Detaching from the mind is the key to perceiving the sprawling present beyond.

Once we abide in this space, the comparing mind does not intervene to check whether we are really in the present or not; whether we are really having the experience that we have read or heard about or not; whether it is comparable to any previous experience that we've had. It is a state of no-mind. We simply live, experiencing every moment in its raw, natural form without comparing it with anything that has been.

Watching the movie of life

When we watch a movie on the screen, many of us tend to lose ourselves in the melodrama. We identify with the scenes and characters and experience the emotions that the characters go through.

For some time, we tend to lose awareness that it's just a movie; we ride the highs and lows of the story.

If we were to watch the movie from the director's standpoint, we can derive a new perspective of the purpose of certain scenes. Why has the director introduced this scene? How does he wish to bring a twist in the storyline? How will this scene lead to the next? With the director's viewpoint, we will be able to enjoy the movie on a different plane, regardless of whether the scenes are tragic or comic, mundane or suspense.

What we learn from this is that we can adopt the director's viewpoint even with the story of our own lives. We can enjoy every scene that has been scripted into our life story, if we adopt the director's standpoint.

But who is the director of your movie? Is it your parents and family, or colleagues at the workplace? What if you were to awaken one day and realize that you are the writer, the editor, the protagonist, the producer, the director, the hero, the villain, and also the audience of your own movie!

When this realization dawns, you can then playfully participate in your life movie. You will clearly see that the current scene of your life is only the preparative precursor to the next scene. Without this perspective, one tends to be lost in the obvious superficial aspects of the scene of life, swirling like a dry leaf that is caught up in the wind currents of the life movie.

We need to train ourselves to observe the happenings, relationships, and the feelings that arise in response from a higher standpoint. For this, we need to be attuned to the invisible script that is being played out as this life. What prevents us from doing so is our ignorance and non-awareness.

Being in the space of the present helps to transcend the vagaries of the life movie and gain this higher perspective. In turn, looking at life from this higher perspective makes it all the more possible to dwell in the untouched bliss of the present.

8

The Treasure Trove of Happiness

Now is where happiness lies. Now is the happiest moment there is.

We often come across these words, but have we truly grasped how deep their meaning is? Firstly, the message that these words convey, is an absolute and unequivocal truth, and once we've grasped its essence, we would always want to stay in the present.

Let us understand its profoundness with the help of an analogy:

> *A guru once visited a forest with some of his disciples. The forest was unusual in the way that every tree in the forest bore a number. When they were well within the forest, the guru turned to his disciples and said, "My dear students, each one of you has been assigned one tree, under which you will find a bag of diamonds. It will also be a wish-granting tree and will fulfil all your wishes. However, I will not tell you which one of the many trees in this jungle is the one assigned to you. To know that, you have to keep playing with this ball." Saying this, he gave each of his disciples a wooden ball and left.*

The puzzled disciples didn't have much else to do, so they started playing with the ball. Some of them being less patient than others, were soon tired of playing with the ball. So they gave up the game and sat down to rest. Some got busy watching others play the game. Some got busy talking and chatting among themselves. A few patient ones however continued to play with the ball and so it happened that after a while, almost all the disciples got busy doing everything else except what they were told to.

Soon, the few who continued playing noticed to their surprise that the wooden surface of the ball was wearing off as they played with it and the worn off surface revealed a number. It also became logically evident that the more one played with the ball, the faster the number would be revealed. After a little more playing, they also noticed that the ball contained some seeds that kept falling out through cracks that had developed on the worn out surface of the ball.

It finally dawned upon them that the number that the ball revealed was in fact the number of the tree that had been assigned to them. They rushed to find their trees and unearth the buried treasure under it. The tree also fulfilled all their wishes as the guru had predicted. The disciples returned to their guru and thanked him profusely.

In this analogy, the forest represents our life and the ball represents the present moment. As we traverse through our life, we have to be with the present moment, live it, enjoy it as much as we can. The "playing with the ball" which is an analogy of enjoying the present moment, has to be constant and uninterrupted. We all wish for prosperity, health, relationships, happiness, peace and tranquility, but instead of looking for these things in the present moment (which is where they are surely to be found), we are busy either reminiscing the past or obsessing over the future.

In short, we are being like all the disciples who chose to keep the ball aside and got busy with worthless activities. By not playing with the ball, we are delaying the revealing of the number that will take us to our wish-granting tree.

The revelation of the number, the finding of the tree, the hidden treasure and the fulfilment of wishes, tells us how living in the present not only gives us the spontaneous joy that comes from playing a game, but also holistically solves all of our problems and fulfils all our wishes. In other words, it lays the foundation of a wonderful future.

The tree gives us the diamonds of health, prosperity and harmonious relations. By not playing with the ball, we never get to know the number and hence stay deprived of the wish-granting tree. Thus, by not being in the present, we are not only deprived of the joy it brings, but also of a wondrous future.

Seeds of the past

The analogy talks about seeds that keep falling out of the cracks in the balls as the disciples play with it. Let us understand what this means. The seeds are those of our past. The ball that represents the present moment contains seeds of the past.

It is interesting to know that we are always carrying seeds of our past, that should ideally be discarded, because if we were to sow these seeds in the present, the future will only yield the same past that has bygone.

In the analogy, as the disciples play with the balls, the seeds keep falling off. This indicates that by being in the present moment we are also keeping our past from getting projected onto our future. We are breaking the cycle; disrupting the repetition. The more we play with the ball of the present moment, better the chances of the seeds of the past getting completely discarded, leading to a novel and amazing future.

The future is in the present too

We often hear people say, "Someday, when all my wishes are fulfilled, I shall be happy!". A student thinks, "Someday, I will graduate with an excellent score and have a fantastic job with a great salary and then I shall be happy!"

All these people are thinking that they will be happy in the future upon the fulfilment of some wish. The missing link that they need to grasp is that happiness is not where they think it is. Happiness is not a result of the fulfilment of wishes; rather, it is the cause.

By choosing to be happy in the present, they are guaranteeing the fulfilment of their wishes. If you sow the seeds of the past in the present, that is exactly what you will reap in the future too.

By sowing happiness now, you are guaranteed to yield the same! By not indulging in playing with the ball of the present moment, you could end up with the wrong tree (an undesired future) that will lead to undesired manifestations, bringing sorrow.

The understanding that the present moment contains both - the seeds of the past and the manifestations of the future - will make us want to always be in the present.

Where does your happiness lie?

There are three ways in which people perceive happiness. When asked, "Where does your happiness lie?", we can expect three answers:

The first answer: "When a certain wish of mine will be fulfilled, I shall be happy." Such people believe that their happiness lies in the future.

The second answer: "My happiness lies in whatever I have today. The house, however modest; the vehicle, however small; the relatives, however few; and the money, as much as there is; is what gives me happiness."

The third answer: "My happiness was in the belongings I had in the past; the wonderful experiences that I have had in the past." Such people think their happiness was in the past and that they have lost it, never to get it back.

We have to contemplate which one of the above is our answer. Our real pursuit of happiness will begin only when we have ascertained where it lies today. If it lies in the future or the past, that goes on to tell us that we haven't realized the importance of the present moment. Contemplating upon this question will bring the urgency to learn to be in the present, because we now know that the present is where happiness truly is.

9

Relinquishing the Past

While we traverse through life, we unknowingly tend to gather packets. Let us understand what these packets are with the help of an example.

When we eat a burger or observe someone eating one, we will notice as one bites into it, the salad and the patty held between the 2 buns, tends to come out of the sides. It has to be pushed back inside before taking the next bite to keep the stuff from falling off. So the act of eating a burger involves eating it and pushing the patty and the salad in, at the same time.

We deal with incidents in a similar way. We face the incident and at the same time push in old experiences, emotions and thoughts that it induces.

When an incident occurs, it arouses memories of past experiences and consequently the emotions and thoughts associated with them. To these, we add our current assumptions and beliefs and stuff this packet of unresolved emotions back in. We gather such packets throughout our life, filling up our mind with sorrow and negativity.

We often come across people who have the habit of stashing away every little thing, however worthless. Such people are have-nots, who are always gripped by the feeling of scarcity. They feel the necessity to stash away everything, thinking they might need it someday. Such peoples' closets are stuffed with worthless belongings. New things keep entering the closet without a single one ever leaving it.

Likewise, there are people who stuff their minds with packets of old experiences and emotions, turning it into a mental museum of antiques, which then becomes the cause for the antics of the mind!

Let us consider another example to deepen our understanding about packets:

Some children were playing in the rain. One of them found a little worm that he put into a small packet and kept it in his pocket. The little worm shrivelled into a curl in the packet.

Whenever the boy would get the worm out of the packet and blow over it, the worm would straighten itself and wriggle. This became an entertainment for the boy. Every time he met someone new, he would get the worm out of the packet and show them how it wriggled, putting it back in his pocket after the demonstration.

Soon, for the lack of sufficient air, the worm grew weaker. This time, when the boy blew over it, it wouldn't wriggle as much as it did before. The boy, thinking that the worm will surely move again some day, kept the worm back in the packet.

A few days later, the boy found the worm dead. He started hunting for other worms that he could play with. He soon started spending a lot of time gathering various insects in his pocket.

This example is about a boy who is trying to find something to entertain his mind. We tend to do the same with dead experiences. We collect them and keep them stashed away in our minds, unfolding them every now and then, vainly attempting to re-live them in our minds, trying to breathe life into them.

Whether the old experience is a happy or a sad one, we keep re-experiencing the same thing over and over again in our minds. What is wrong with that, is that while re-experiencing an old and dead experience, we are missing out on the happiness of the present moment. Out of ignorance and unawareness, we are letting the experiences of the past adulterate those of the present. To understand this adulteration, try a little experiment:

You will need two water buckets for the experiment. Fill up the first one with hot water and the second one with warm water. Now, first dip your hand in the first bucket that contains hot water. Hold it in there for a few seconds and then dip the same hand into the second buket that contains warm water. You will observe that the water in the second bucket, although warm, feels cool to the hand.

Why does this happen? Why does the warm water feel cool to the hand?

This happens because the skin of the hand, the sense of touch, is still carrying the packet of its past experience with the hot water. This past experience causes adulteration of the new experience in the present with the warm water. The experience of the hot water tampers with the experience of the warm water. This goes on to indicate how an experience of the past keeps us from fully assimilating an experience of the present, depriving us of the truth; deceiving us into believing warm water to be cool.

If we were to drink tea after having chocolate fudge, the tea will naturally taste bland. Does that mean the tea is truly tasteless? No! The tongue is still carrying the experience of the fudge, due to which the tea tastes so.

Imagine if the tongue had carried the experience of everything it has ever tasted?! Nothing we would taste in the present would have any taste! Everything would taste bland and tasteless. Thankfully the tongue lacks this ability of holding onto past tastes. However, that is not the case with the mind. The mind adheres to the experiences of the past, ruining the present one.

Likewise, in life we tend to view every person, thing and incident through the glasses of our past experiences. For example, whenever we meet a person with whom we have had an argument in the past, the same experience, emotions and thoughts surface every time we see the person or even if the person is mentioned in a conversation.

This is due to the packets we collected when the incident first happened and kept them stored in the mind ever since. The experience need not always be a bad one. The same applies to a happy experience as well. Any experience, however happy or sad, is a thing of the past and has to be relinquished.

Peter had visited the snow-clad alps in Switzerland and was awestruck by the natural beauty. This pleasant experience was stored in his mind and had become a packet that he was unfolding every few days and re-living for a short while in his mind's eye. This seemed okay as long as it wasn't hampering his experiences in the present.

The following year, Peter and his friends planned a visit to the nearby hill station just outside his hometown, as they did not have the time or budget to make a long distance trip like that to Switzerland. When they reached the hill station, they checked into the hotel and then rushed to a famous sunset spot.

However, when they reached the spot, Peter unknowingly began unfolding the packet of his experience in in the Swiss alps from the previous year and started feeling disappointed and dissatisfied with the beauty of the present location. For him, it didn't match the splendor of Switzerland. While his friends were enjoying the breathtaking scenery of the orange sunset before them, Peter was sulking about how this place just wasn't good enough and how his money had been wasted.

Peter's indulgence in a past experience, although a happy one, was depriving him of the joy of a perfectly good experience in the present. We often come across people who have the habit of reiterating their experiences to anyone who would listen to them. Reprising their troubles and misfortunes gives people a sense of satisfaction.

We have to let go of these packets or we will soon find that the past will have such a deep impact on the present, that it will completely dominate the present. While trying to derive false and shortlived happiness from past experiences and memories, we are deprived of the happiness and benefits of the present.

Relinquish the experiences of the past

We derive good or bad experiences from the incidents that we encounter in our lives and these become packets that we stash away. Later when a similar incident occurs, based on these packets, we mentally re-live the same old experiences all over again. These packets stop us from perceiving and accepting the present moment with a fresh perspective. They are obstructions to what the present moment has in store for us. Instead of making the most of the experience of the present, we waste time by comparing it with our past experiences.

Consider a person who goes to a movie theatre to watch the sequel of a movie that he has already seen. While he sits down to watch the new movie, he is thinking, "The first part was just brilliant! Would this sequel be just as good? Is it possible that it will fail to match the excitement that the first movie created?"

Although he is in the movie theatre to see a new fresh movie, he is really expecting a repetition of the same old movie. This constant comparison leads to disappointment, as it stops him from fully enjoying the fresh experience that the new movie is meant to give him. If he were to enjoy the sequel without any comparison to its predecessor, we can consider his mind to be truly free of packets, at least with regards to the movie.

Relinquish the tendencies and instincts of the past

> *Bill was the son or a very poor farmer. He had always seen days of extreme financial struggle. His poverty was a great source of sorrow and stress for him. He would borrow money from people and would often lie to them about returning the money.*

His sorrow had also turned him into an alcoholic. Every evening, he would be doused in alcohol ridden stupors. Without any concern for his health, he would drink till he dropped down every evening, worsening his situation, both physically and financially.

After having spent many years in poverty, Bill came to know one day that he was actually the son of a very wealthy businessman. He came into possession of great wealth and all his woes about his financial wellbeing disappeared overnight! He was now so rich that he barely had to do anything and he could still afford a lavish lifestyle. And yet, every evening he would feel the irresistible urge to get drunk.

When he was poor, he would drink to numb his sorrow and frustration about being poor. However, even though he had become rich, he continued to feel the urge to drink alcohol because it had become a habit. Every evening, his past emotions and instincts would play out and he would find himself holding a glass of alcohol.

Every now and then, he would have bouts of realization that he wasn't poor anymore and he would give up his drinking, but the addiction was so strong, that he would soon relapse.

Every time Bill lost sight of reality, he would go back to repeating his past behavior. Likewise, we too tend to collect and store experiences and emotions in the form of memories and compulsive behaviour. Every time we unfold and re-live these memories, we are repeating our past.

It is time to relinquish all such memories, compulsions and behavioral tendencies that are rooted in the past.

Experiences of the mind and the Experience beyond the mind

There are two distinct kinds of experiences we have: first is the kind that our mind has and the second is the kind that our true self has. We're not talking about experiencing the mind and the self; we're talking about what these two experience.

The unique experience that comes from meditation is in reality an experience of the true self, who we truly are, beyond the mind; it is experienced by the real Self. However, the mind steps in and takes credit for the experience. "I was the one who experienced this!", it says and then turns the experience into a packet and stores it.

Consider an expert pianist, who is rendering a symphony on the piano. When his performance reaches its peak, the pianist is lost in the performance. He does not exist at that time. All that exists is the performance, the brilliant rendering of the symphony. However, after the performance, the mind steps in and takes credit by saying, "I performed so well!" It also stores this experience and refers it for comparison with subsequent performances.

It is often very difficult for us to distinguish between what was experienced by the mind and the experience beyond the mind; and this is the very art that we have to acquire.

The experience of the real Self, or in other words, the *transcendental experience,* is always available in the present. This experience shifts us into the present, bringing all our focus on the feeling of havingness in the present moment. It elevates our awareness and gives us unadulterated and everlasting happiness.

Experiences of the mind are like wells of pseudo-happiness that lure and trap us. The sooner we get rid of them, the better! We have to relinquish them completely.

Letting go of both - bad and good

The mind finds it comparatively easier to relinquish so-called bad, negative and unwanted experiences. However, it is challenging is to get the mind to relinquish even the so-called good ones. An experience, however good or bad, is a thing of the past and is dead. Hanging on to it for too long is only going to be harmful for the present and the future prospects contained within the present moment.

We gather many experience in any given day. However, instead of collecting these packets, surrender them and face every new day with a clean slate. While we put on our shoes every morning to go out, let us tell ourselves, "From now on, every time I leave the house, I shall do so with the understanding that I have surrendered all my packets and am leaving with a fresh new perspective of everything that I am going to come across!". Only when *both* the good and the bad packets are surrendered, will we be able to truly enjoy the present.

Letting go of packets of past knowledge

Often, out of ignorance, we also make packets from the scientific and intellectual knowledge we have acquired. There is no worse misuse of any knowledge than that which prevents us from welcoming new knowledge! These packets hinder our quest for knowledge in the present too. We even disapprove and reject novel ideas and knowledge that come our way, due to these accumulated packets. We have to train our mind to receive and assimilate knowledge as it is, without adulterating it with what we have gathered in the past.

In spite of several beings attaining the state of self-realization and stabilization in the experience of the true Self in the past few centuries, scientific intelligence refuses to accept the existence or even the possibility of any such state! This is because people have strong packets (set perspectives) regarding science and hence refuse to acknowledge any different perspective.

If one were to argue with an atheist about the existence of God even for a whole day and if the atheist were to hold onto his past packets of experiences, he would still end saying, "You are wrong. There never has been and never will be a God."

Even when it comes to the subliminal topic of the existence of God, people have packets that they strongly adhere to. Hence, it becomes difficult to make someone who does not believe in the existence of God, change his mind about it.

The highest use of the human intellect lies in recognizing and acknowledging its own limitations and being open to the profoundness of reality that exists beyond its understanding.

Hence, before we can begin to assimilate wisdom and knowledge with a new perspective, we need to understand everything about how packets are formed in the first place, else we will always tend to compare the new with the past, thereby blocking the acceptance of anything new.

How are packets formed?

Do you remember the first time you experienced a solar eclipse? Remember how you felt excited! You had ran up to the terrace or out on the street with your solar eclipse glasses or a bunch of X-ray sheets to view the eclipse. The day had turned to night in a matter of minutes. All this was new and you didn't know what would follow.

Now try and imagine the time when a solar eclipse was experienced for the very first time by humans. Was there the same happy excitement that you yourself had felt during one? The bright sun had suddenly disappeared and all was dark in the middle of the day! People must have been so scared.

Deceptive astrologers and religionists must have led people to believe that the disappearance of the sun was a result of the wrath of gods and asked them to perform rituals and sacrifices to appease them and ensure the return of the sun. People, who were driven by fear, must have followed the word and performed the rituals and sacrifices and then the sun appeared again! This cemented their belief that the rituals and sacrifices were the reason for the return of the sun.

Today as people with scientific minds, we know the real reason of this phenomenon. But many religions continue to follow the tradition of performing certain rituals during eclipses. These superstitions and illusions are the packets that have been handed over through generations, stopping people from enjoying a great natural phenomenon.

It is hence necessary for us to get rid of packets - good or bad - so as to assimilate new knowledge and wisdom.

10

Breaking Free from Karmic Bondage

Imagine a man who lives in a prison cell. After a hard days labor at the prison camp, he comes back to his cell and scratches a line on the wall. These lines tell him how many days he has spent in prison and how many more he still has to. Why does he feel the necessity to ruin the clean walls around him by scratching lines all over them? Why spoil the surroundings that he lives in? Now take a minute to think whether we too tend to do the same?

Yes, we do!

By misbehaving, ill-treating and hurting the people around us and those we come in contact with, on a daily basis, we are creating karmic bondages. This is similar to the man defiling the walls in the analogy above. The prison cell represents the past and the future that we tend to lock ourselves in. We fail to understand the importance of staying in the present, all the time drifting into the past or the future, and often end up creating these karmic bondages with people in our lives and degrading our surroundings. This spoils not only the ever important present but also the prospective future.

The more bondages we form, the farther we drift from liberation. The goal we are working towards is to attain liberation during this very life, while we are alive. People assume liberation to be something that can only be attained after one's death. This myth has to be annihilated with the understanding that death is only the end of our physical existence. Our journey continues beyond the physical realm and liberation can be attained while we live, by assimilating the wisdom of the ultimate truth. This is analogous to the man breaking free from the prison cell.

Suffering grief that never was

We get attached to our past, finding it difficult to surrender it while the future is something that hasn't manifested yet. The present is the moment in which we find ourselves swaying towards either of these. Our present is stale and overshadowed by our past and this is the reason for the sorrow and grief that we suffer.

Consequently, it becomes evident that the grief we suffer from, was never made for us in the first place. It is our own tendency; our own behavior that leads us to it.

> *Tanya heard from someone that some guests were going to visit her. She became restless and worried about the preparations she would have to make. She felt frustrated at how her daily routine had been disturbed because of this unexpected visit. She felt tired even thinking about attending to the guests, serving them food and showing them around the town. After spending a tense day, she came to know in the evening that*

the guests were to stay at someone else's home, not at her house. Tanya had spent a whole day unnecessarily suffering torment that wasn't meant for her at all. She was just misinformed and that so quickly turned into her grief.

Even if we are faced with sorrow or troubles, there are ways in which it can be dealt with instead of feeling bogged down by it. The following example illustrates this point:

Phil was told by his doctor to drink a glass of bitter gourd juice every morning. This had become a great distress for Phil. He had started dreading the mornings because of it. After trying hard to get used to the taste, he finally called upon his doctor and asked him if there was an alternative to drinking the juice. The doctor prescribed a tablet that provided the same benefits as the juice, and Phil breathed a sigh of relief.

This shows how there are often alternatives in situations that help us deal with them without having to feel sorrow. However, due to the lack of knowledge about the alternatives, we keep drinking the bitter juice of the past and spoiling the beauty of the present moment.

It is not that we are completely unaware of the importance of living in the present. Every religion, every culture is full of teachings about this and yet we find it difficult to actually assimilate it into our lives. The experiences of our past keep shadowing our present and that not only affects our present but also creates a future that is a projection of the past.

All the incidents and ordeals that a person encounters since his childhood, become suppressed injured memories, which are stored as packets that keep accumulating in his mind. Lack of affection and attention from parents, betrayals by friends and loved ones, all such incidents and the emotions arising from them like anger, anxiety, grief etc. get amassed in the mind and it becomes like an active volcano. Any small trigger causes an outpour of these emotions, spoiling the present and often leading to creation of even more karmic bondages.

The vision of the person gets clouded by rage, guilt, conjecture and distrust making him blind to the present moment and the potential it holds. This deprives him of happiness and the present moment begins to feel dull and insipid. To be able to stay in the present, he has to learn to relinquish the past and everything therein.

Memories and expectations - Our undoing

Our mind has a weakness for thoughts; it cannot do without them; it feeds and thrives on them. In fact, thoughts are what the mind is made of. Consider the following example:

> *Roy came back from his very first morning walk feeling invigorated, refreshed and energetic. He met John on his way to his apartment and told him what a great experience he had had and urged him to give it a try.*
>
> *Inspired by Roy's words, John made up his mind to take a morning walk himself. He set out early next morning, all the time analyzing whether he was having the same experience as described by Roy. After about a hour, John returned home feeling quite disappointed.*

Why was John disappointed? You will notice that John constantly kept comparing his experience with that of Roy's. The packet of Roy's words was stuck in his mind and he kept comparing it with his present experience, which deprived him of the happiness that his walk could have given him. This illustrates how preconceived notions and assumptions obstructs us from fully enjoying something in the present.

An astrologer once told a travelling trader, that he would meet with an accident during his visit to one of the towns, within a year. Imagine the traveler's state of mind after being told this pseudo-prophecy! Whichever town he visited, he would wonder whether this was the one where he would finally meet his fate. He continued to feel suspicious about every town and village until the year was over. Every trip he undertook in the year after his interaction with the astrologer, was stressful.

The anxiety to know the future ruins our present. To keep the present pure and unadulterated, we have to learn to welcome every incident and person with a fresh perspective; unblemished by the taints of the past or the anxiety of the future. The mind will habitually tend to unfold packets but we have to remind ourselves, "I welcome whatever this moment holds for me with a clean slate. I am witnessing this incident, meeting this person for the first time ever and shall not have biases based on packets."

Try going for a walk every morning as if you are doing it for the first time. Meet every person as if you are meeting them for the first time. Laugh at a joke as if you just heard it for the first time. Assimilating this understanding in every little thing we do will bring about a huge change in how we experience life.

11

The Happiness of the Present

Imagine that you have received two gifts from someone. While you grab the first gift to open it, your mind draws your attention to the second one, thinking, "What could that one contain?!"

With the chapters we have gone through so far, we have enough understanding of the importance of the present to be able to tell the mind to focus on the first gift first. "The second gift is an experience and happiness of the future. Let me first open the first gift which is what the present is all about."

With this attitude, we will notice that every day, every moment unfolds a new wonder; a new adventure in our life. This can never happen if one falls prey to the whispers of the mind.

Even if something positive and pleasant is happening now, the mind, instead of letting us enjoy it, would want to peep into the future in the anticipation of knowing how better it gets there. It is like someone failing to enjoy a movie in the anticipation of what the climax would be.

Consequently, by never staying in the present, a person fails to experience what he could have, never trains the mind and finishes his earthly journey never having truly lived! A popular adage says, "Man lives as though he is never going to die, and then dies as if he had never lived!" This is so true. It is hence imperative to learn to be in the present to make life worthwhile. Keep asking yourself, "What does the present moment hold, that I could be failing to see?" Perceive every subtle thing that the present wants to convey and do not let any illusion overshadow you.

A person enters a cinema hall after seeing a poster of a comedy movie at the entrance, expecting the comedy movie to be playing inside. However, upon entering he finds that the movie that is actually playing is a different one and isn't a comedy. Now this person is sitting there, waiting for the comedy movie to start, assuming that the one playing now isn't as good or as enjoyable. This is all that he is thinking about throughout the movie, never thinking of enjoying whatever is playing at that moment; never knowing all that he is missing.

While we sulk about not getting what we expected, we miss out on what we are getting in the present. What a wastage it would be if we were to squander all our life, all the time thinking about the future!

Scripting our life in the present

We often make the mistake of wallowing in things of the past or the future. People who have the habit of writing a diary about their everyday life and experiences, share an observation that while writing, their mind often tends to sway either forward or backwards. They are at times thinking about what has been written or about what is to be written.

Consequently, due to their lack of focus on what they are writing at any given moment, they make mistakes. They do not, however, realize that they have made mistakes.

At the end of the writing, they feel they have correctly written everything they wanted to. It is only when they go back and read what they have written that they realize their mistakes. They learn from these mistakes as they move ahead. This prospect is applicable only to those who indulge in self-examination and introspection.

Those who do not have the habit of introspection are like those students who write just as much as necessary for them to get the examination over with and escape the hall. In the hurry to get it over with, they make silly mistakes that could have easily been avoided, but they're busy thinking about finishing and running away. They do not want to spend quality time in the examination center, making sure what they have written is correct and precise.

Even if such people are told that there is still more than an hour to go before the exam ends, they will still not want to wait. They are not used to being in the present, and hence are blind to all the mistakes they are making. If that hadn't been so, they could have corrected a lot of mistakes and learned valuable lessons from them; which in turn would have guaranteed a better future.

12

Evaluating Packets

A person wanted to sell his ten year old car, so as to buy a new one. When a buyer approached him, he told the buyer that he would sell it at the same price that he had bought it ten years ago!

This is obviously an absurd request. The seller is expected to demand the present day depreciated price of the used car, which would be lesser than the original one.

Let us contemplate on the inference of this analogy: if the value of a commodity is re-evaluated on a daily basis, shouldn't the same also apply to incidents, experiences and memories? If we are giving them the same value as (or probably even more than) the first time, we are going wrong!

The time and energy that we spend brooding over anything has to be according to its present day value, which should be - at the least - far lesser than the original value. Ideally, it shouldn't have any value at all, because anything that is from the past, as long as it is not a lesson, is worthless.

Let us consider another example to understand this better:

> Some friends had met up one evening after many years and were discussing their lives. Soon, the nature of what they were sharing began inclining towards the negatives. They began reiterating the challenges and disasters they had faced, their disappointments about their relatives, their colleagues and other acquaintances.
>
> One of the friends, sensing the direction in which the evening was headed, got up and declared that he was going to tell a joke. After he was done telling the joke, everyone laughed out aloud, and people got back to talking about their lives.
>
> After a little while, the same friend got up again and repeated the same joke. This time he just got a mild response from his audience as a few people chuckled at the joke while others wondered why he was repeating the same joke.
>
> After a little while, he stood up again and repeated the same joke for the third time! This time, no one laughed. They all just stared blankly at him.
>
> The friend smiled and explained his conduct. "My friends," he said, "If hearing the same joke can't make you laugh the second time, why does remembering the same incident make you feel sad each and every time? If the humor in a joke depreciates every time it is repeated, why shouldn't the sorrow associated with a memory depreciate too? Why can't we wipe out the past and move on with life with a clean slate?"

The greatest accomplishment on the path of spirituality is getting rid of the vacillating and comparing mind. This is the source of all sorrow and burden we feel. It compares everything with something from the past - that is all it does. Even if one is feeling happy, the mind will compare it with the happiness felt in some past experience, and then infer that the present happiness isn't as great.

For example, if a person is celebrating a festival, the mind, instead of enjoying the proceedings, will compare the celebrations with the previous year's celebrations and lose out on the happiness of the present.

While we are learning about taking things as they are in the present without any comparison, the least we can do to get on the path is to start experiencing afresh, the griefs and sorrows that the present situation brings. Usually the grief in the present is accompanied by packets of the past, that magnify it beyond its real quantum. If we were to perceive the negativities in their real magnitude, we will notice that we overestimate their intensity.

If we are to grieve over something, let it just be the grief of the present, not accompanied by that of the past. Re-evaluate how much grief comes from the present and how much of it comes from something that has happened before. By doing this, we have to free both our joys and our sorrows from the clutches of the past. Let us look at an example to understand this better:

> *There was a bird, which like any other bird, loved flying freely in the open sky. It would fly over beautiful forests and rivers, stooping down every now and then to catch insects and worms to fill its stomach.*
>
> *The bird however, had a curious habit. Every time it felt sad, it would pick up a little black stone and a white one every*

time it felt happy. These stones were kept in a little bag that the bird had sewn out of some leaves. The bird would carry the bag wherever it went, holding it in its claws.

Naturally as days went by, the number of stones increased and it became increasingly difficult for the bird to stay in the sky. The bird however, not only refused to give up the stones but also continued to collect more.

Eventually the bird had to give up flying for the fear of losing the stones. It now stayed in one place, all the time guarding the stones, never leaving the bag alone. It would only catch the insects that came close to the bag, so it started starving as well.

Finally one day, the bird died out of thirst and hunger, and the only thing that remained behind as a memory of the bird, were the bag of stones!

We need to sincerely look within ourselves: Are we too living like this bird, making the same mistakes? Have we too forgotten the glory of flying freely in the skies of joy and wonder, being obsessed with our own bags of memories?

People collect traumatic memories and negative impressions. They re-live them again and again, staying chained to them until they die. There is no freedom for them, unless they themselves realize how these packets are keeping them bound and that they need to let them go.

Familial packets

Many people say that it is hard to forget their first love. And everyone else agrees with them. But has anybody given a thought as to why this happens? With the first love, they had no previous packets of that experience. Hence, they simply loved that experience in its uniqueness. But then they created such packets that any following experiences seemed bland thereafter.

This habit of holding onto past packets can cause so much frustration that it can even lead to breakups. People break apart and look for love in new associations. But again, the same thing repeats and they continue to believe that the fault lies in the people. They hop from person to person, but never realize why they got to experience pure love in the first place. It was because the mind was empty without any past packets!

The purpose of having relationships in life is to be able to help each other grow and live happily together; to bring about the mutual understanding and enjoyment of the bonding between two people. However, people horde packets of hate, anger, disappointments and frustrations for their family members. Due to this, neither of them are able to benefit from the relationship. The true purpose of relationships is lost and what remains is a sense of vague and indifferent acquaintance.

Repressed packets pack so much negativity in them that they can become extremely explosive in nature. They can explode any time without any warning and cause the complete extermination of the relationship between two people, beyond any hope of revival. The solution to this is to be transparent in relationships.

If people were able to be transparent; that is to say if they were able to calmly and compassionately communicate their honest feedback, opinion, or point of view to one another, instead of mutely suppressing their feelings, their relationships would be much more successful and beneficial to everyone involved. This is only possible through mutual understanding and cooperation. Neither sides of a relationship can or should assume an unyielding position.

Choosing pleasant and positive words while talking, humility and empathy go a long way in repairing relationships before they are pushed beyond a point of no return. We have to use these qualities to handle relationships, and not let our packets govern our outlook towards others. Experience relationships after casting away past packets and notice how they seem much more pleasant and enriching.

Some people not only horde packets themselves, but also pass them on to others.

> *On her first day as a teacher at a school, Tara was to replace Emilia as the class teacher. She asked Emilia her feedback about the class. "My god, that class is notorious!" Emilia exclaimed, "turn your back on them for a second and they will wreak havoc! You better be strict and stern with them!"*
>
> *Tara entered the classroom carrying the same image that Emilia had given her of the class and treated them very strictly. The children in the class, finding the new teacher to be the same as the old one, continued to respond in the same old way, thus confirming Tara's already biased opinion about them.*

In this example, Emilia passed on her packets to Tara, who instead of deciding for herself, decided to take someone else's words for it. Because of Emilia's words, Tara went on the offensive, being overly strict with the kids, which was unnecessary. Had she treated the kids with compassion and love, the children would have perceived her as being different from their other teachers and cooperated by being understanding and docile.

Having packets will almost always lead to fear or hatred about others. As against that, if we were to interact with people openly, compassionately and positively about what we expect of them or what we think of them, people will want to trust, listen and oblige. Everyone wants to hear sweet words and no one likes being talked to harshly. This simple understanding can be used to harvest great relationships.

13

Dealing with the Past and Future

Imagine a hypothetical world, where every newborn baby is made to inhale a special kind of gas that enables the baby to instantly grow up to any age of its choice. For example, as soon as a baby is born, it inhales the gas and instantly grows to 25 years of age, as per its wish.

However illogical and absurd this may sound, try and imagine it for the sake of an experiment. Use your heart, not your head to understand the next few lines.

Now imagine yourself to be a part of this world. You too have have been born just now, inhaled the gas and instantly grown up to your present age! Although your physical appearance is exactly as it is right now, but within, you are essentially a newborn that has no past experiences or impressions at all. Even if you were to try to mentally go into the past, you wouldn't be able to, because you have no past! You are just born right now.

Imagining this scenario rewards us with a valuable lesson. It can help us break the vicious habit of getting stuck in the past.

This does not mean that we have to completely obliterate our past or escape from it. There are valuable lessons in there that we have to remember. The visit to the past has to be short and only intended to revise those lessons so as to improve our conduct in the present. We end up doing the very opposite of this; we get stuck in the past, re-living the experience and emotions associated with it.

However, our subconscious mind is not able to distinguish between an experience of the past, and that of the present. For it, everything is in the present. For example, when one sees a dream, one's subconscious mind is fully convinced that whatever is happening in the dream, is the reality. Whatever we project on it, it believes that to be the reality.

If we were to re-live past memories, our subconscious mind perceives them to be the present and re-create similar consequences, making us go through similar incidents all over again. In such a situation, we have to remind ourselves, "The past, however good or bad, is dead."

Visiting the past and the future

After reflecting on all that we have read so far, if one still feels like revisiting one's past, one should do so like Superman. Superman has the ability of flying anywhere at supersonic speeds. This is exactly how we should visit our past. Instead of taking a leisurely stroll, we should make it quick and snippy.

The only justified reason for visiting the past is to learn from past experiences; to revisit the lessons that we had learned and to re-evaluate what we should be doing differently now. There could be precious lessons there that we missed.

Once we have placed our wallet in the cupboard or our car keys into our pocket, we stop worrying about them because we are convinced that we have placed these things in the right and safe place.

Likewise, once we have learned the lesson that a certain incident had to convey, we should stop worrying or obsessing over it because once the lesson is extracted, whatever remains in the past is dead. For this reason, every time we want to visit the past, we should fly in and back as fast as possible; like Superman; to save ourselves from getting stuck in the mire.

Similarly, visiting the future should be done like Spiderman. Spiderman has the ability to shoot webs from his palms, helping him swiftly navigate himself in specific directions. While visiting the future, once we have ascertained the action plan and set goals to be met, we should get right back to the present, without continuing to linger in the future, obsessing over the plan and its outcome.

The best way to plan for the future is to write down all the tasks and actions. The burden that we feel when faced by many tasks, is usually just because we are thinking too much about the tasks, rather than actually performing them. Our mind seems to be full of tasks that need to be attended to. Even the thought that so many tasks are pending, overwhelms us and affects our productivity.

In such a scenario, we should list all the tasks on paper. When we list things, we get them out of our mind and onto a paper. By doing this, we are emptying and unburdening the mind. Getting things out on a paper puts a stopper to all the thoughts about our pending tasks, making us feel lighter in the head. Now we can start working on the list with an empty mind that helps derive heightened productivity.

So, the best reason to visit the future is to plan your actions and the best way to visit it is like Spiderman - with full control over our sense of direction and time.

When one lingers in the past or the future, one is empowering one's vacillating mind; allowing it to take over. The mind plays the pivotal role in taking you away from the present and keeping you away. The present is the one place where it can be silenced. We should hence practice the art of being in the present - the only place where the vacillating mind can be made powerless.

We can practice meditation to learn to stay in the present. Meditation helps us slow down our thoughts, eventually stopping them entirely. With the thoughts gone, there remains nothing for the mind to do and we enter a transcendental state beyond the realm of thoughts. Being in this state not only helps us harness the full potential of the present, but also builds a wonderful future.

Repetition of past choices

Imagine a person who goes to a certain restaurant and orders the same dish every time. Although the dish he orders is of his liking, there are many other dishes that the restaurant offers that are just as good, probably even better. But he wants to stick to the one dish he has tried before and doesn't want to change his order.

The human mind is like this person. Once it likes a certain experience, it repeatedly wants to order the same thing over and over again. It makes packets of such experiences and keeps them safe, to re-live them again and again. Nature, however, in it's infinite creativity, has many myriad experiences that it wants us to have, but understanding this is beyond the capability of the mind. It will keep playing the same memories again and again like someone watching the same movie over and over again.

Sowing the right seeds

Our present is a direct result of the seeds we have sown in our past; the prayers we did. If someone is not happy about their present situation, they need to make a quick visit into their past to understand what went wrong while they were sowing.

We can look at the present, to understand the mistakes we have done in the past, and then consciously, based on these lessons, sow the right seeds now, to reap a wonderful future. Contemplate over what changes we need to make in ourselves today, so that we never have to suffer for a single day of our life, hereafter.

14

Bringing Completeness

Imagine that one fine day you wake up in a strange place where things change every second. For example, you keep a cucumber in the fridge and find a tomato in its place the next day. You keep a pen in a box and find a pencil in its place the next day. You keep a bookmark in a book and you find a clip in its place the next day. You slide a pizza into the oven, and out comes a burger. Everything changes and you're perplexed!

While you're figuring out what's happening, you notice some people who seem to be very happy. You ask them how they can be so happy in such a place, only to get a surprising reply. You find out that their happiness is owing to the fact that they have accepted the situation. They have accepted the fact that they will never find the same thing in the same place ever, so they have learned to make peace with whatever they find in its stead. They have given up their desire of finding the same thing that they had kept in a certain place the previous day.

You are however perplexed and disappointed because you desire to find the same thing that you had placed. The happy people tell you that you will not find peace until you accept the changes, like they did.

While this analogy describes a farfetched place, it actually points at the world within us. It throws light on our tendency to expect things to work out in the same way as before. We expect people to behave in the same exact manner as always. We expect the outcome of a certain task to be the same every time. However, people, situations, everything keeps changing and we find it difficult to accept these changes. We refuse to look at things the way they are in the present.

When we resist something, it is as if someone has tied one of our hands behind us and we're trying to solve the problem with a single hand. By not accepting, we're inconveniencing ourselves.

It is not being said that one has to just blindly accept whatever one is facing and not do anything about it. On the contrary, by accepting the situation first, we are untying the hand that was tied behind, and now we can work on the problem with both our hands.

When we accept the changes happening in everyday life, we are immediately shifted to a higher place of being; a higher level of awareness, from whence we get guidance about what the next step has to be. When we're resisting, we're in a negative and restrictive frame of mind. In such a state, one cannot resonate with the potential of the present.

The importance of completeness

The reason we keep drifting into the past or the future is because there is something in there, that is giving us a feeling of incompleteness, a feeling of lack. One who has failed at achieving a certain goal that he had set for himself, feels incomplete due to failure. This incompleteness keeps pulling him into the past. Most people are unaware that incompleteness is the real culprit and that it needs to be resolved.

To resolve the incompleteness one feels about the regrets of the past, one has to develop acceptance. Only by accepting whatever has transpired, can one attain a sense of closure. Once that happens, one will find it easier to stay in the present. The very hook that was pulling one into the past disappears.

There are people who feel incomplete about their future as well. For example, a person believes that he can be happy only when he visits Paris. Until he is able to make a trip to Paris, he lives with this incompleteness. His happiness depends on the trip. A person believes that he can be happy only when he owns a luxurious mansion.

We believe that our happiness comes from the fulfilment of desires, and until then we are plagued by the feeling of incompleteness. The key to finding completeness with our future is to understand the true meaning of happiness and whence it comes from.

Due to our mistaken belief that happiness comes from external objects and situations, we ceaselessly direct our attention and efforts towards the external world. Desires are incessant streams of thoughts that seek fulfillment from worldly objects or situations. Whenever a certain desire is fulfilled, the restlessness of the mind caused by that desire subsides temporarily. This allows us to experience the happiness that always exists within us, but for a short while.

Imagine a brick wall, every brick of which, represents a desire we have. Every time a desire is fulfilled, the brick that represents that desire, disappears making a hole in the wall. Through the hole, we are able to see what lies beyond the wall; the experience of the true self, the source of happiness. This is the happiness we experience upon the fulfilment of a desire. However, soon another brick (desire) appears in place of the one that had disappeared, filling up the gap in the wall, obstructing the happiness beyond it, yet again.

Thus, we fail to recognize that the happiness that we experience is already present within us. We wrongly connect the happiness that was experienced with the objects of our desire. The more we experience such momentary happiness, the more convinced we are that we can obtain happiness from people, objects and circumstances outside ourselves. Hence, we continue to desire those things that we believe to be the sources of our happiness. This, at the cost of losing the ultimate source of happiness that is always available within us!

The missing link here is that desire, in itself, is never the cause of sorrow, or the lack of happiness. It is the habit of chasing our desires, based on the belief that happiness lies in their fulfillment, that causes sorrow.

And we never doubt that we are living as a victim of this illusion because we see everyone else around us living this way. When everyone is plagued by the same disease, it doesn't seem like a disease; it is rather assumed to be a norm.

Understanding the true nature of happiness and seeking happiness where it can truly be found (within us) will dispel the illusion of future expectations that we ride on. This can bring completeness in the present for things that we were postponing for the future.

Part III

Harnessing the Present for a Fulfilling Future

15

Intuiting the Future

We all wish for a glorious, bright and prosperous future. However, not everyone is able to manifest the future that they dream of. Great creations are possible when one is being properly guided. But where do we get the guidance for creating the future that we wish for? How do we know what are the right actions to be taken today, to manifest the future we want?

The answer lies within!

Intuition is the guidance that comes from within. Let us understand how intuition functions with an analogy of a radio. The radio broadcasting center is continuously transmitting radio programs. For us to be able to receive the broadcast on our radio, we have to tune into the right frequency. It would be wrong to assume that the radio is not receiving the broadcast because there is nothing being transmitted. That would amount to blaming the transmission for the fault in the radio.

Likewise, we are continuously receiving guidance from within, in the form of intuition; but we have to tune into the right frequency to be able to receive, decode and decipher it.

We have all experienced the spark of intuition at some point in our lives. For example, while we are thinking of a certain person, we receive a call from the very same person. We feel a strong feeling inside about some impedance. These are the most common examples of intuition at work. By tuning ourselves, we can begin to harness the power of intuition.

The ability to intuit is present within everyone. It is just that some are more attuned to it, while others rarely pay heed to it. The common question that many people ask is how the power of intuition can be developed. Here are some steps on how to develop your intuition and use it to ascertain the right things to be done in the present:

1. Recognize when the message is being communicated

We are constantly being provided with intuitive guidance. If grasped well, it can tell us exactly what needs to be done at any given moment. This guidance can be in the form of a spoken word, or a signboard, a book we read, the words of a song we hear. They may not even be as clear as these examples.

Communication from within can often be very subtle, like a feeling, a hunch, a fleeting image. Guidance can also come in the form of a physical sensation like uneasiness in the stomach, goosebumps or a feeling of sudden relief. Sometimes, if the messages seem too obscure, we can ask for a clearer one. In this way, we can tune ourselves to the right frequency to receive the guidance from within.

2. Ask for specific guidance

If one is looking for guidance for a very specific situation or dilemma, one can ask specific questions to receive answers from within. But having asked for guidance, it is also equally important to get into the receiving mode to get the answers. That is where meditation comes in.

3. Practice meditation

If prayer is the question, then meditation is the answer! Prayer is only half the magic. Meditation completes the magic. People focus on prayer, on creative visualization and subconscious mind techniques. But they miss the all-important need to meditate. You ask for something through prayer. But then you have to be in silence to receive the answer. In other words, being in meditation makes you receptive and attuned to the creative principle, so as to receive what you have prayed for.

Practicing meditation regularly helps detach from the constant noise of thoughts in the head and shift to the serenity of the heart. Even spending 10 to 15 minutes consistently at the same time every day can deepen ones attunement with the heart and develop the ability to recognize when intuition speaks.

4. Write down the answers

Messages arising from intuition are subtle and can fade out of one's awareness within seconds. Hence, it helps to write down the insights that arise as quickly as possible, lest they are lost. When we write down these flashes of insight, we are indicating to nature that we are open to receive and serious about acting on them.

We can maintain a journal for recording the guidance for ten minutes daily. This practice is a way of strengthening the power of intuition. When this is consistently practiced, we will marvel at the clarity of what comes through from the heart.

Our decisions will arise from the place of boundless wisdom, which cannot be matched by any level of rationale or analytical reasoning.

5. Let the heart choose when to use the head

Acquiring guidance from the heart does not mean that we should not put our analytical reasoning to use at all. The intellect is a tool that can be used to plan effectively and evaluate alternatives and outcomes.

However, when should the intellect be used? For most people, the thoughts in the head takeover their lives. Their attention is invested in their thoughts to such an extent that they rarely dip into the heart and seek guidance. However, when we hone our power of intuition, we learn to abide in the heart and allow our life to be directed from within.

This also means that the intellect, or the reasoning mind can be effectively used, provided it is directed from the heart. When the heart suggests the use of the intellect, then we can use it by all means.

The other by-product of relying on the thoughts in the head is that the personalized ego takes credit even for innovative ideas that arise from the heart. This limits the flow of ideas, as the ego draws boundaries and personalizes everything.

When we understand that the body and mind can be an effective medium for the most creative ideas to manifest, we will begin to live in receptive gratitude for the guidance that comes from within.

6. Recognize the inner voice by noting telltale signs

How do we become more familiar with the voice of intuition within us? Besides following all the other steps mentioned earlier, we also need to note telltale signs that act as signposts.

Suppose that you are meeting a stranger and he appears very convincing and trustworthy. However, you go by your gut feel and decide not to deal with him. You then meet your friend and discuss about the stranger. Your friend says, "You're in luck that you didn't proceed with him. I know people who have complained about his integrity."

Now, your gut-feel was actually sounding warning bells. The consequences prove that your inner voice was guiding you. When this is so, you should try to recall and reflect on how exactly you were feeling when you were conversing with the person. What were the body sensations that you felt? Was it a heaviness or uneasiness in the stomach? Or a sore sensation in the chest? Or was it just an unexplainable feeling of discomfort or an unknown fear?

Note these telltale signs in your journal. Verify them across many such occurrences. With this, you can refine your sensitivity to the inner voice, as you would be learning its language.

7. Take prompt action

When we act sincerely and promptly on the guidance we receive from within, we begin to receive even more guidance that is specific and easier to decipher. Faith is the key to action. When we trust our intuition and act, we begin to harmonize and synchronize our life with the higher guidance.

Whether we want to make better decisions or solve problems effectively, we will observe that our intuition is working miracles, the more we trust it and act upon it, thereby shaping a bright future.

16

Receiving Past Parcels Gracefully

What goes around, comes around.

This is a famous maxim that points to the law of karma. But, what does karma mean? It means that whatever we do, with our body, speech, or mind, will have a corresponding result. Each action, even the smallest, is pregnant with its consequences. Even inaction has its own consequences. When something goes wrong in our lives, and we are unable to figure out why it happened, it can be bewildering.

> Raj was about to cross the street on the way to his office when he noticed an aged man, who was also trying to negotiate the traffic to cross the street. Seeing the old man hesitating, Raj felt sorry for him and offered his hand to help him cross the street.
>
> After crossing the street, the old man jerked Raj's helping hand off and walked away without exchanging any pleasantries or words of gratitude. Raj was taken aback by his ungrateful response. He said to himself, "The old man is so uncultured... He could have at least said 'Thanks', if not bless me... Uncivilized fellow!"

Now, does the help rendered by Raj constitute a good karma or a bad karma? The answer to this question will determine the kind of future that his karma will beget.

The missing link in understanding this is what constitutes karma. Our actions are not merely what we speak or do. In truth, it is primarily what we think or feel that determines the quality of our actions. Our feelings and thoughts are actions too, much more than our words or actions.

Mental actions, in the form of thoughts and feelings, are the primary determinant of the quality of karma; outward physical action comes later. What may seem to be a terrible act to your eyes could possibly be backed by the purest intention. On the contrary, what may seem to be the most benevolent and kind act could be a crafted manifestation of a wicked or selfish intention.

It is the thoughts and feelings that we entertain behind any action that acts as the seeds for our future. When Raj offered a helping hand, his intention was pure. But when the old man walked away thanklessly, Raj was angry within, though he did not express it outside. This was because his desire to be acknowledged or appreciated was thwarted.

Despite performing a benevolent act, Raj's mental reaction to the way the old man responded plants negative seeds for Raj's future. This is true, even though this may not be acceptable to many people.

This means that we need to be consciously aware, not just about our external actions, but also our mental responses to the daily happenings around us.

Gracefully receiving parcels

When people respond in ways that we don't like, we feel hurt or angry. This is because we don't see that whoever we deal with is only delivering a parcel that was actually due to us. As per the law of karma, the seeds that we've planted in the past, mature and manifest in our lives. This manifestation can be considered as a parcel that is being delivered to us. It was due to us anyway.

Nature has only chosen a particular person through which the parcel is being delivered to us. But here's the catch. When we are ignorant of the way nature is settling our past karma through such parcels, we react negatively to the one who delivers us the parcel. The parcel may be an unpleasant one, but we have the choice of accepting it gracefully or reacting negatively. By reacting negatively, by fretting over it, or being angered and blaming people around us, we are making matters worse by planting further seeds for our future.

By gracefully accepting whatever nature delivers to us through various situations, we are reconciling and clearing our past karma, without planting further recurrences for the future. However, to do this, we need to be vigilant in the present moment, when we are faced with testing situations.

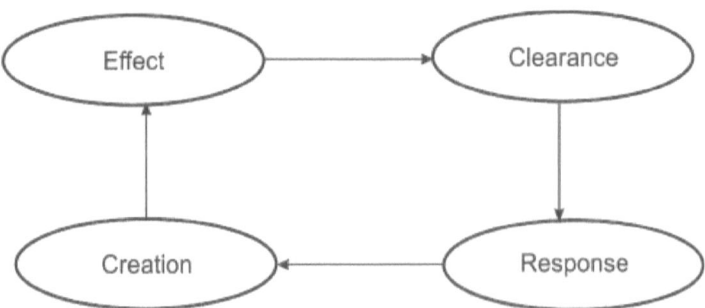

The above diagram indicates the four steps that constitute this process. When an external event triggers a perception within us, it has its effect. This effect leads to a particular experience, pleasurable or painful, which is a form of payback. It is the fruit of the seeds of karma, planted in the past. This also leads to clearance of the karmic cycle, unless we react in a way that plants further seeds for the future.

If we lack awareness in the present and are ignorant of the way nature functions, we will behave as a victim to this effect. We then react impulsively and plant the seeds for further recurrence of karmic payback. Thereby, we unconsciously create an undesirable future for ourselves.

In the earlier example, if Raj had the clarity of how nature delivers karmic paybacks through everyday incidents, he would ignore the cold response of the aged man and be grateful that past karmic seeds are being reconciled through the incident. By doing so, he could have planted the seeds for a life of joy and freedom. He only needed to be alert about the thoughts and feelings that were arising within him.

If we are alert and make a choice to receive this effect gracefully, then we will respond positively to the situation. With a response that comes from such higher awareness, we settle the karmic account and plant the seeds for a brighter future – a future of true freedom.

17

Formula-based Actions

We have a tendency to create a formula for everything, and then to try using the same formula to derive the same result every time.

Consider a few simple examples:

A person feels happy and satisfied after eating a pizza followed by ice-cream, the first time. So, pizza + ice-cream becomes his formula for happiness. Now, every time he wants to feel happy, he thinks he should have pizza followed by ice-cream.

A manager in an office wanted to get some work done from his subordinate. So he yelled at him and the subordinate completed the task. So, yelling at people to get work done became this person's formula. He would use this formula everywhere to get his work done.

People try to achieve things by adopting immoral and unethical ways, and if they succeed, that becomes a formula for them. For example, a student cheated for the first time in an exam by copying answers from his fellow students, and got a good score. So, cheating to get good scores becomes a formula for him. He will now cheat in his exams instead of sincerely studying for it.

When we achieve success, we tend to unconsciously develop a success pattern based on it. We try to repeat the same old success patterns, believing that they will continue to yield success in the future too. However, our past success formula could possibly become a deterrent in trying new ways of achieving success.

This formula-based approach often works for failures too. A person who did not fare well at his first interview, carries the experience of the failure into his second interview. He is already on the defensive even before the interview starts. His heart beats are elevated and he loses his spontaneity and alertness. As a result, he fails in the second interview too. During the first interview, he had an open mind and a fresh approach. However, fear got the better of him during the second one.

Parents use the age old method of scolding and even giving children a beating to make them understand something. Spouses blackmail each other to get the other to agree to something. Supervisors are harsh with their subordinates at work. These are all examples of formula-based behavior.

Why do we have this tendency? Because we resist change. We want to find a way in which we can get assured results each and every time. Once we've found the way, we prefer to stick to it. Even when we realize that a particular method is not yielding results any more, we still try and persevere with that method.

Some people spend all their lives doing everything the exact same way, never changing at all. In the process, they do not realize that they are living the same old days again and again. Life has stopped for them. They try to escape anything that would mean changes in their fixed life pattern.

We also have the tendency of sticking to old patterns because we like to stay in the comfort-zone of what we already know and are uncomfortable about stepping into the unknown. Being in the present is about allowing life to unfold without holding onto preconceived ways or fixed expectations.

Breaking free from formula-based actions

The first step towards breaking this tendency is to become aware of one's actions in the present. When we look at our actions with awareness, we will be able to analyze when we are indulging in formula-based behavior. When we becomes sensitive to the signs, it becomes easier to spot when it is happening.

The second step is to ask ourselves, "Do I want to respond or act in the same way as I did before?" By pausing to contemplate over this, we will realize that our actions in the past were based on our understanding of that time. Situations may have changed since then and the same action may not be necessary or even appropriate anymore.

Let us resolve to bring a change – however small – in every routine action. For example, a homemaker may change the way food is cooked every day, or the way the house is cleaned. If the vacuum cleaner was operated with the right hand, use the left hand instead. A working professional may introduce novelty to the way he schedules, tracks and reports his tasks.

This serves two purposes: Firstly, to think of new ways and changes, we have to tap into our creativity, which requires all our focus. This makes it easier to stay in the present, keeping all our attention engaged in the task. Secondly, introducing creativity into everyday routine and mundane tasks brings joy.

The same can be applied to the way we interact with people. Find new ways to greet them when you meet. Let it become your signature that you never greet the same person twice in the same way. The wonderful thing is, when we begin tapping into our creativity more and more, it starts flowing and newer alternatives will spring up within us.

There are often many different ways to do a certain task, but we always choose to use the same way we did the first time. Let us change our choice. This simple change can bring about a huge shift in our lives.

18

Starting from the Finishing line

If you were to tell a child, "Go and play outside for some time, and I will gift you a box of chocolates." What would the child say? He would be surprised – getting to play outside is a gift in itself. What more could he ask for!

The child doesn't need a gift or anything in return to play. Playing is a gift for him; his joy lies in playing. Playing, in itself, is joy for the child! Why would he expect anything in return?

But when it comes to the game of life, do we play it for the utter joy of it!? With every activity that we engage in, our interest lies in what we will get out of it. Most often, it is the fruit of action that motivates us, more than the action itself.

The best dancers immerse themselves into their art to the point where they do not identify themselves as separate from their art. When they are dancing on stage we may see it as a person dancing flawlessly, but to them the only thing on stage is nature taking its course. There is no person. There is no ego.

If only we could live in the moment and derive joy from our actions. If we gain the perspective of playing the game of life, then we will participate in every activity sportingly. With such a playful attitude, the beneficial results or consequences of our actions would become mere bonuses. Our actions would be an expression of joy in themselves!

Nothing will then seem difficult, for all the so-called difficulties will be challenges that we welcome. Challenges make the game more interesting to play. We would be truly living a life of freedom if we didn't need any additional motivation for action. Action is motivation!

The trouble with acting from expectations

While negative deeds bear negative consequences, virtuous deeds need not necessarily bear good consequences. Instead they could bear a mixed bag of both happiness and sorrow. If you hold expectations of admiration or other gains in return for your actions or you consider yourself righteous because of your good deeds, then your streak of happiness is destined to hit the wall of sorrow eventually.

Sure, good deeds bring a fulfilling feeling of righteousness. But if you find yourself attached to such feelings, then any impedance in their flow can shake your world. You cannot be possessive of something that is temporary in its very nature. If you are possessive about acquiring and preserving what you gain from your actions, then the smallest of slumps will take you down the spiral of sorrow. Therefore, good deeds are not the means to an end in themselves. We must aim beyond good deeds to selfless deeds that are devoid of expectations.

If you are not attached to the fruits of your actions then it makes them selfless. To give an example, when you bathe every day, you do not do it for want of admiration. In fact you do not expect anything in return because the very act of cleansing yourself is a fruit in itself!

Cleanliness is your very nature. When you live by your very nature, you do not expect anything in return. So when we do not expect praise in return for bathing, why must we expect it in return for cooking meals, or earning a livelihood for the family, or doing well on a project at the workplace?

If you cook a meal with creativity, love and pure intention, then you have already reaped the fruits of your actions, regardless of the praise you may receive for it. If however, you feel disturbed or offended if not praised, you would not only be postponing your joy, but also making it conditional. Your joy would then be subject to the responses of others.

Immersing yourself in action

Whether you are cooking a meal in the kitchen, or working in the office, immerse yourself in it. There are many such examples that personify selflessness. Why do we remember Mother Teresa? Because she was immersed in selfless service. There was no desire for anything in return. If there was a selfish desire, then such noble work wouldn't even begin.

When a dancer is at the peak of the dance performance, the dancer is immersed in it, such that she ceases to be a separate entity. She has become one with the dance. All that remains is the dance. When this happens, the performance reaches the highest expression.

So it is with every activity that we engage in. When you immerse yourself in it, when you become one with it, the quality of the action is raised. There is no separate 'you' that would expect anything in return for the action. Then the action itself is the reward for you.

Sometimes we do find ourselves immersed in the moment for the joy of it, while listening to music or while dancing. We love going on vacations because it is easy for us to forget ourselves in the lap of nature. We need to bring similar feelings into all our actions.

Playing for the sake of playing

When you participate in a running race, you run to win. Your aim is to cross the finishing line before anyone else does. Your happiness does not lie in the starting position; you see it far away – beyond the finishing line.

But what if you were to start from the finishing line? You participate in the race because you have already won! You run because you are happy. The consequence of the race does not really matter to you, for you are already experiencing the joy of touching the finishing line at the very beginning. For you, running itself is joy. You play for the sake of playing, not winning.

What has happened here? Here, you are not acting to gain joy. You are already in joy, and action arises from joy! Let us understand this further.

We have been programmed to believe that we can gain happiness through whatever we do. And we continue believing this without doubt because we see everyone else around us in the same pursuit. This makes us seek happiness in the world.

The world can never bring us lasting joy. Doing something cannot bring us joy. Action is not the means to joy. True action flows from joy. When we truly understand this profound truth, we will stop playing the game of life to win. We would have overcome the illusion of the pursuit for happiness.

True happiness lies in simply being in the present. It is like the sunlight that lights up everything merely by its presence. Everything on earth springs to life owing to the presence of sunlight. What does the sun do for all this? It is just present. All activities proceed in its presence.

By understanding the essence of the present and practicing to abide in it, we can revel in the pure untouched joy of our true nature and shape a fulfilling and productive future.

■■■

You can send your opinion or feedback on this book to :

Tej Gyan Foundation, Pimpri Colony, P. O. Box 25,
Pimpri, Pune – 411017 (Maharashtra), INDIA
email : mail@tejgyan.com

Write for Us

We welcome writers, translators and editors to join our team. If you would like to volunteer, please email us at: englishbooks@tejgyan.org or call : +91 90110 10963 or +91 90110 13207

About Sirshree

(Symbol of Acceptance)

Sirshree's spiritual quest which began during his childhood, led him on a journey through various schools of thought and meditation practices. His overpowering desire to attain the truth made him relinquish his teaching job. After a long period of contemplation, his spiritual quest culminated in the attainment of the ultimate truth. Sirshree says, **"All paths that lead to the truth begin differently, but end in the same way—with understanding. Understanding is the whole thing. Listening to this understanding is enough to attain the truth."**

Sirshree is the author of several spiritual books. His books have been translated in more than 10 languages and published by leading publishers such as Penguin and Hay House. He is the founder of Tej Gyan Foundation, a not-for-profit organization committed to raising mass consciousness by spreading "Happy Thoughts" with branches in the United States, India, Europe and Asia-Pacific. Sirshree's retreats have transformed the lives of thousands and his teachings have inspired various social initiatives for raising global consciousness.

His works include more than 100 books and 3000 discourses. Various luminaries and celebrities such as His Holiness the Dalai Lama, publishers Mr. Reid Tracy and Ms. Tami Simon and yoga master Dr. B. K. S Iyengar have released Sirshree's books and lauded his work. 'The Source' book series, authored by Sirshree, has sold more than 10 million copies in 5 years. His book *The Warrior's Mirror*, published by Penguin, was featured in the Limca Book of Records for being released on the same day in 11 languages.

Tejgyan... The Road Ahead

What is Tejgyan?

Tejgyan is the existential wisdom of the ultimate truth, which is beyond duality. In today's world, there are people who feel disharmony and are desperately trying to achieve balance in an unpredictable life. Tejgyan helps them in harmonizing with their true nature, the Self, thereby restoring balance in all aspects of their life.

And then there are those who are successful but feel a sense of emptiness or void within. Tejgyan provides them fulfillment and helps them to embark on a journey towards self-realization. There are others who feel lost and are seeking the meaning of life. Tejgyan helps them to realize the true purpose of human life.

All this is possible with Tejgyan due to a very simple reason. The experience of the ultimate truth is always available. The direct experience of this truth is possible provided the right method is known. Tejgyan is that method, that understanding. At Tej Gyan Foundation, Sirshree imparts this understanding through a System for Wisdom – a series of retreats that guides participants step by step

Magic of Ultimate Awakening Retreat

Magic of Ultimate Awakening is the flagship self-realization retreat offered by Tej Gyan Foundation The retreat is conducted in two languages – Hindi and English. The teachings of the retreat are non-denominational (secular).

This residential retreat is held for 3-5 days at the foundation's MaNaN Ashram amidst the glory of mountains and the pristine beauty of nature. This ashram is located at the outskirts of the city of Pune in

India, and is well connected by air, road and rail. The retreat is also held at other centres of Tej Gyan Foundation across the world.

Participate in the *Magic of Ultimate Awakening* retreat to attain ageless wisdom through a unique simple 'System for Wisdom' so that you can:

1. Live from pure and still presence allowing the natural qualities of consciousness, viz. peace, love, joy, compassion, abundance and creativity to manifest.

2. Acquire simple tools to use in everyday life which help quieten the chattering mind, revealing your true nature.

3. Get practical techniques to access pure presence at will and connect to the source of all answers (the inner guru).

4. Discover missing links in practices of meditation *(dhyana)*, action *(karma)*, wisdom *(gyana)* and devotion *(bhakti)*.

5. Understand the nature of your body-mind mechanism to attain freedom from tendencies and patterns.

6. Learn practical methods to shift from mind-centred living to consciousness-centred living.

For retreats contact +919921008060 or email: mail@tejgyan.com

A Mini retreat is also conducted, especially for teens (14-17 years) during summer and winter vacations

MaNaN Ashram

Survey No. 43, Sanas Nagar, Nandoshi gaon, Kirkatwadi Phata, Sinhagad Road, Dist. Pune 411024, Maharashtra, India.

About Tej Gyan Foundation

Tej Gyan Foundation (TGF) was established with the mission of creating a highly evolved society through all-round self development of every individual that transforms all the facets of his/her life. It is a non-profit organization founded on the teachings of Sirshree. The foundation has received the ISO certification (ISO 9001:2015) for its system of imparting wisdom. It has centres all across India as well as in other countries. The motto of Tej Gyan Foundation is 'Happy Thoughts'.

TGF is creating a highly evolved society through:

- Tejgyan Programs (Retreats, Courses, Television and Radio Programs, Podcasts)

- Tejgyan Products (Books, Tapes, Audio/Video CDs)

- Tejgyan Projects (Value Education, Women Empowerment, Peace Initiatives)

TGF undertakes projects to elevate the level of consciousness among students, youth, women, senior citizens, teachers, doctors, leaders, organizations, police force, prisoners, etc.

Now you can register **online** for the following retreats

Maha Aasmani Niwasi Shivir
(5 Days Residential Retreat in Hindi)

Magic of Ultimate Awakening Retreat
(3 Days Residential Retreat In English)

Mini Maha Aasmani Shivir
3 Days (Residential) Retreat for Teens

www.tejgyan.org

Books can be delivered at your doorstep by registered post or courier. You can request for the same through postal money order or pay by VPP. Please send the money order to either of the following two addresses:

WOW Publishings Pvt. Ltd.

1. Registered Office: E-4, Vaibhav Nagar, Near Tapovan Mandir, Pimpri, Pune 411017.

2. Post Box No. 36, Pimpri Colony Post Office, Pimpri, , Pune 411017

Phone No. : 9011013210 / 9623457873

You can also order your copy at the online store:

www.gethappythoughts.org

*Free Shipping plus 10% Discount on purchases above Rs. 300/-.

For further details contact:

Tejgyan Global Foundation

Registered Office:

Happy Thoughts Building, Vikrant Complex, Near Tapovan Mandir, Pimpri, Pune 411017, Maharashtra, India.
Contact No.: 020-27411240, 27412576
Email: mail@tejgyan.com

MaNaN Ashram:

Survey No. 43, Sanas Nagar, Nandoshi gaon, Kirkatwadi Phata, Sinhagad Road, Tal. Haveli, Dist. Pune 411024, Maharashtra, India.
Contact No.: 99210 0 8060.

Hyderabad: 9885558100, **Bangalore:** 9880412588,
Delhi: 9891059875, **Nashik:** 9326967980, **Mumbai:** 9373440985

For accessing our unique 'System for Wisdom' from Self-help to Self-realization, please follow us on:

	Website	www.tejgyan.org
YouTube	Video Channel	www.youtube.com/tejgyan
facebook	Social networking	www.facebook.com/tejgyan
twitter	Social networking	www.twitter.com/sirshree
	Internet Radio	http://www.tejgyan.org internetradio.aspx

Online shopping
www.gethappythoughts.org

Please pray for World Peace along with thousands of others at 09:09 a.m.

www.ingramcontent.com/pod-product-compliance
Lightning Source LLC
LaVergne TN
LVHW041851070526
838199LV00045BB/1546